BLACK BOOK
OF
HORROR

Selected by Charles Black

Mortbury Press

Published by Mortbury Press

First Edition

2012

This anthology copyright © Mortbury Press

All stories copyright © of their respective authors

Cover art copyright © Paul Mudie

ISBN 978-0-9556061-8-2

Mortbury Press
Shiloh
Nantglas
Llandrindod Wells
Powys
LD1 6PD

mortburypress@yahoo.com
http://mortburypress.webs.com/
http://twitter.com/mortburypress

Contents

Dedicated to Christine Campbell Thomson
1897-1985

*****

Acknowledgements

The Anatomy Lesson © by John Llewellyn Probert 2012
The Mall © by Craig Herbertson 2012
Salvaje © by Simon Bestwick 2012
Pet © by Gary Fry 2012
Ashes to Ashes © by David Williamson 2012
The Apprentice © by Anna Taborska 2012
Life Expectancy © by Sam Dawson 2012
What's Behind You? © by Paul Finch 2012
Ben's Best Friend © by Gary Power 2012
The Things That Aren't There © by Thana Niveau 2012
Bit on the Side © by Tom Johnstone 2012
Indecent Behaviour © by Marion Pitman 2012
His Family © by Kate Farrell 2012
A Song, A Silence © by John Forth 2012
The Man Who Hated Waste © by Marc Lyth 2012
Swan Song © by David A. Riley 2012

Cover artwork © by Paul Mudie 2012

*****

THE ANATOMY LESSON

John Llewellyn Probert

It begins with a girl's scream.

Of course, there have been preliminary arrangements before this. The specimen has had to be prepared, undressed, meticulously washed and then restrained. Then there has been the necessary ritual of demonstrating to the exclusive and very high fee-paying audience that she is healthy and free from disease or skin blemishes, and finally a show made of how very carefully her body has been strapped down to prevent movements that could render the performance a disaster before it has even begun.

But it is the first scream that really signifies the beginning of the performance.

This evening the specimen is in her early twenties and doesn't make a sound until she sees her tormentor approaching the table, clad in the appropriate garb for someone who is about to undertake an anatomical dissection in a living, awake, alert human being. Then she screams – long and loud, and at the same time a shiver of collective anticipation runs through the audience.

The Demonstrator's surgical gown, mask and cap are fashioned from crisp white linen, all the better to show the blood. There is extra protective padding around his neck and wrists, as these are the areas most likely to be bitten at as he goes about his work. He did once toy with the idea of gagging the specimen but he is well aware that screams are what his audience has most paid to hear

The Demonstrator likes to think of himself with a capital 'D'. His real name is, understandably, kept a secret from all but the most personal of his confidantes and business partners. As far as he is aware, the form of entertainment he offers is entirely unique and unavailable anywhere else on the planet. Of course he knows of establishments that offer torture as pornography, as titillation for the uncultured masses, but he prides himself on offering an experience that he considers to be rather different.

The complete dissection of a human being, awake and sensitive to every incision, every cut, every division of tissue, with the specimen concerned taken apart in such a way that they remain alive and aware for as long as is medically possible. Such an undertaking requires skills and a knowledge of the intricate workings of the human body more likely to be found in a surgeon than a sadist. Which is one of the many reasons why the Demonstrator considers himself to be so special.

For he is both.

He looks out over the audience that have gathered in the run down, abandoned theatre that has been arranged to house tonight's very private, very exclusive, performance. A different venue is required each time for obvious reasons and he leaves such organisational concerns to the small group of very loyal and very well paid individuals he has assembled around him to deal with such matters over the last few years.

The girl is currently lying with her left side facing the audience. The table to which she is strapped is capable of a wide range of movement, and may be rotated, elevated, tilted or tipped to give the audience the best possible view of the part of her anatomy on which the Demonstrator is currently working. As is almost always the case, she is very pretty. He always insists that his procurers obtain the most attractive specimen possible. For obvious reasons his audience is always willing to pay more to see a pretty girl dissected instead of an ugly one. Besides a fit slim individual is far easier for him to dissect than some obese wastrel. He rolls his eyes for a second at the memory of the incident a year ago when he had been forced by circumstances to make do with a specimen that must have weighed close to eighteen stone. The audience were nearly asleep by the time he had pinned all the fat back. He looks at the helpless figure beneath his blade and is relieved there won't be such a problem this evening.

He begins with her left lower limb.

The girl screams again, much more loudly this time, as the scalpel blade is drawn down the outer aspect of her left thigh, exposing the attachments of some of the muscles and the glistening nerves that supply them.

As the dissection progresses, the Demonstrator looks up from time to time, gauging his audiences reactions as any good stage performer should and tailoring his actions appropriately. There is always a point at which his spectators will begin to tire of the specimen's screams, when her pointless pleas become more irritating than titillating. This time it takes about half an hour for him to see that the front row are starting to become distracted by her constant cries for help, and this is the point when he picks up the syringe filled with local anaesthetic and plunges it into her throat, just to the left of her trachea and aims the steel needle upwards. He depresses the plunger and the noises she is making subside as her vocals cords become paralysed, reducing her efforts to little more than empty exhalations, as redundant as her attempts to move the hands he has stapled to the wood to stop her from wriggling too much.

He is not planning to preserve her, not this time. No one in the audience has come forward with a sufficient bid to make it worth his while, and if they are unwilling to pay, why should he be willing to prepare for them the ultimate souvenir of their visit? If the appropriate funds had been forthcoming from the two or three individuals who had expressed an interest prior to the performance then he would have placed the spikes not through the palms, but through the wrists in the space between the radius and ulna bones. He had learned through bitter experience that any attempt at securing a body vertically to an embalming board by nailing through the palms results in failure. The human body is too heavy to be supported by the small muscles and tissue layers of the human hand and tearing almost always occurs, leading to collapse of the specimen and damage to the artwork thus produced. But there will be no sale tonight. The body will have to be disposed of in the usual manner.

*

When the show is over the Demonstrator goes backstage. The garments he has been wearing are deposited in a laundry bag, which is then sealed and sent to be incinerated. The shower he uses to remove any blood and tissue that may have adhered to him drains to a tank, which will also be disposed of at a location far away. He dries himself off and then goes into the room next door.

It has been lavishly prepared as per his specific instructions. Even though he intends spending very little time there, he always feels he has earned a small slice of luxury straight after a performance, and even though the mahogany panelled chamber will be stripped after he has left, for this brief moment it allows him to fully unwind as he pours himself a measure of absinthe and takes a tiny sip.

His three-piece black suit has been laid out for him. Once he has dressed he contemplates telephoning his daughter to see how her first week at university has been. He takes out his mobile and for a moment thinks about switching it on before putting it back in his pocket with a knowing smile. It will be much safer to do that when he is back home.

He finishes his drink and, suddenly feeling tired, contemplates sitting for a while in one of the three luxurious leather chairs that have been provided for his comfort. He checks his fob watch. He should really be getting home, especially as he promised he would ring Emma and she will be expecting a call from her Dad. He snaps the watch shut and tucks it away. Time to get going.

It is only when he turns to leave that he realises there is someone in the room with him, standing by the door.

"It's all right," he says, assuming it's one of the men that will have been employed to take the room to pieces once he has left. "I was just on my way out. You can get started clearing all of this up now."

The figure steps out of the shadows to reveal a well-dressed man of about the Demonstrator's age, the black cloak around his shoulders lending him a distinct air of theatricality.

"I'm sorry to disappoint you," the man says in a well-modulated voice. "But I'm afraid I'm not one of your cleaning boys."

The Demonstrator appears nonplussed by this unexpected intrusion. Most likely it is a member of the audience who, having been unable to afford the entire specimen to take home with them, would nevertheless like a little souvenir of their visit.

"If it's an autograph you want," he says, "I am sure you can appreciate my reticence as regards such matters. Similarly, if you are some kind of journalist, please don't even consider the possibility of an interview. In the past twelve months I have been offered more money than any currently popular celebrity, and much as such a considerable degree of remuneration for my simply having to talk appeals, I am well aware that any answers I give might aid those who would do me harm. In particular those who wish to discover my true identity."

The intruder holds out a hand.

"May I reassure you that I am neither autograph hunter nor journalist," he says. "In fact you and I have something in common."

The Demonstrator is reluctant to shake the proffered hand but can find no good reason not to. "And what might that be?" he asks as he releases his grip.

"We are both stage performers," is the reply. "Admittedly that is where the similarity ends. The horrors you display are all too unpleasantly real, whereas my forte is the world of illusion."

"You mean you are a—"

"A magician," and here the Magician, as he likes to be known, gives a deep bow. "At your service."

"And what brings you behind the scenes of my performance this evening?"

The change in the Magician's expression is very subtle, but the hardening of his smile does not go unnoticed by the Demonstrator.

"Why," he says, "merely to have a drink with you." He eyes the empty absinthe glass, "although I fear I may be a little late for that. However I would also very much like to engage you in conversation for a short while. If, of course, you are agreeable?"

The Demonstrator shakes his head and does his best to sound apologetic.

"I'm terribly sorry," he says, checking his watch again to emphasise that he must be going, "but I'm afraid I do have to be somewhere very shortly."

"Yes, but you see," says the Magician, "you won't actually get very far at all unless you do speak to me."

The Demonstrator looks the Magician up and down. Apart from the fact that the man is blocking the door there seems to be little to prevent him from leaving the room.

"I warn you," he says. "One shout from me and there will be several members of security in here who will remove you by force if you do not leave now."

"Well they may be able to get rid of me," says the Magician, removing the cloak and laying it to one side. "But I very much doubt they'll be able to do anything about the poison."

"Poison?"

"Yes – the poison I slipped into your absinthe. And of course you didn't see me do it – I am a magician, after all." The Demonstrator licks his lips but all he can taste is aniseed. He looks down at the glass and as he does so he feels slightly dizzy. Or is it just his imagination? "Whether you believe me or not is of course entirely up to you, but the only way you're going to be able to get hold of the antidote is if you listen to what I have to say."

The Magician draws up one of the luxurious leather

armchairs and positions it so that its back is against the door. As he sits so does the Demonstrator, opposite him and just six feet away.

"What do you want?" The Demonstrator croaks.

From somewhere about his person the Magician produces what looks like a pack of cards. He shuffles them expertly and, displaying them in a fan presents them, face down, to the man opposite him.

"Pick a card," he says. "Any card." The Demonstrator hesitates. "There's no trick," says the man opposite. "Not in this part of our little talk, anyway."

The Demonstrator reaches out, and takes one from somewhere near the middle of the fan of cards. As soon as he takes hold of it he realises that they aren't cards at all, but old-fashioned Polaroid photographs, turned face down.

He is not sure he wants to know what is on the other side.

"A nice touch, don't you think?" says the Magician. "No one's used Polaroids for years but I thought it would add a little something." His voice suddenly loses its warmth. "Turn it over," he says.

The Demonstrator does as he's asked. At first, he has some difficulty working out what the picture is meant to be of. He is reminded of a sea creature pushed into a tank too small for it, or perhaps a rubber manikin that has been squashed away for storage. And then he realises.

It's a girl.

The container into which she has been forced is clearly too small for her, and her thighs are pressed so tightly against her chest that she must have difficulty breathing. Her splayed out fingers have caused the tiniest spots of mist to form on the surface of the glass. Which means she must still be alive. Or she was when the picture was taken.

"Now don't let me look at it," says the Magician. "Just put it back in the pack."

What else can the Demonstrator do? He slips the photograph back in amongst the others.

11

"I shall now find your card for you," says the Magician, back in performance mode. He shuffles the pack, takes out one of the photographs, and holds it up to his captive audience of one.

"Is this your card, sir?"

The photograph he has picked shows the same girl but from a different angle. Her face is pressed so hard against the constricting glass that it is impossible to make out individual features. Her blonde hair is damp and knotted.

The Demonstrator shakes his head. Where is this going?

The Magician looks at the card and pretends surprise at picking the wrong one.

"Well that's never happened to me before," he says. "But then that's usually because I make sure that the entire pack consists of the same card. I know I'm not supposed to let you know how such tricks are done, but in this case, this very special case, I'm intending to tell you everything."

He throws the pack on the table before the Demonstrator, who can now see that each photograph shows a different aspect of the same girl, crammed almost impossibly into the tightest of glass jars. When he looks closer at the picture that has fallen nearest to him, he can see that her hands and feet are already blue from her compromised circulation, and the lid is probably so tight that the air that is allowing condensation to form on the glass next to her mouth won't last very long at all.

"Your work?" says the Demonstrator, raising an eyebrow but appearing otherwise unmoved. The Magician nods. "Then perhaps you can explain to me how the skills of a contortionist might be attributed to your good self?"

That elicits a grin.

"Quite simple," says the Magician. "The girl in that picture is not a contortionist. In fact, you won't believe how difficult it was to squeeze her in there."

"And then I suppose you made her disappear, did you?"

The Magician pauses and for a moment stares at his black patent leather shoes. "No," he eventually says. "Not exactly.

12

Although in general I am very good at making things disappear. Very good indeed." He stares at the Demonstrator knowingly as if this is supposed to mean something. When no response is forthcoming the Magician leans back in his chair and says in as offhanded a manner as he can manage "like your daughter, for instance."

Now he has the Demonstrator's attention.

"What do you mean?"

"Exactly what I said," says the Magician. "Your daughter Emma has, for want of a better word to describe it, disappeared from society and has been auditioned for a job as a contortionist."

The Demonstrator tries to rise from his chair but finds he cannot. His arms and legs have become lead weights and he can barely shift his torso to lean forward as he rasps from swiftly paralysing vocal cords, "What have you done with her?"

"Well I haven't killed her, if that's what you're thinking," says the Magician, getting to his feet. "Although goodness knows I should have, after what you did to my Sally."

The Demonstrator tries to repeat the girl's name but now all he can manage is a croak.

"You won't remember her name because I'm sure you didn't ask it," says the Magician, moving the chair away from the door. "Just as I'm sure you never ask the names of any of your victims. Because let's face it that's what they are. I know you don't consider them to be that, but then I very much doubt you even consider them to be human. Just specimens for you to take to pieces, raw material for you to demonstrate your art upon. Well in spite of that, somewhere in your twisted soul you must have harboured the worry that one day your sins would catch up with you."

The Demonstrator cannot move at all now, and his breathing is becoming laboured. But he can see. As the Magician edges the door open he can see something waiting behind it. Something in silhouette, hunched over and breathing heavily.

13

"Quite a large girl my Sally was," said the Magician. "And surprisingly enough that was what led me to you. An overheard conversation from one of your dissatisfied customers in a Monte Carlo bar where I was performing a month ago and I knew it was you the police were looking for. Well they shan't have you. Not alive, anyway." There is a pause and the merest hint of a smile in his voice amidst all the bitterness. "They can have your daughter though, if they like. I was totally honest with you when I said I hadn't killed her, you know. What I wasn't totally honest about was how good a magician I actually am." While he has been talking the Magician has been edging out of the room. Now he moves round behind the shadowy hulking shape. He rests his hands on the top of the heaving bulk as he continues. "You remember that old trick about sawing a woman in half?" The Demonstrator can neither nod nor shake his head but merely strain his eyes to see what it is the Magician wants to show him. "Well I was never terribly good at it you see. The sawing part, yes. I was remarkably good at the sawing part. It was the putting them back together again that I could never really get the hang of."

And with that the Magician takes his leave, but not before giving the shape before him an almighty shove so that it all but falls into the room.

The Demonstrator, his heartbeat now so rapid and his breaths so shallow that the room is already dimming, strains to look through a blur of tears at the thing of horror that is trying to crawl towards him, and his consciousness begins to fade the last thing his dulled ears ever hear is probably the word:

"Daddy."

THE MALL

Craig Herbertson

Bailey pushed his way to the front of the escalator queue. It was Christmas Eve; he felt sick and wished it would all end. The unrelenting consumers seemed unusually irritating. Someone stood on his toe. A bag crammed with bulky toys hit him in the stomach. There were no apologies for the series of assaults on his person. It seemed the accepted thing that one risked insult and injury on this most religious of holidays. Holidays? That was a laugh. Over-commercialism, greed and crass vulgarity had seen it off years ago. Christ! He could remember when shops closed on Saturday afternoon and Sunday was a day of rest as it was meant to be.

Somehow he broached the escalator, only to find he was going the wrong way. The cryptic note written by his wife and purportedly containing directions to some awful toyshop dropped from his hand in a crumpled ball. Bailey watched it fall and roll down the steps. He'd probably never escape this living hell.

At the top of the escalator he ducked an outstretched hand and by some genius manoeuvred his weary body to an oasis of relative calm. He needed a break but the open café, over-lit with glaring lights, seemed packed full of the living dead. Did anyone enjoy this? A glance at the worn out faces and the slouched bodies of the men was a clue. Bailey was pretty sure they didn't. Those with kids seemed utterly at the end of their tether. One or two of the women's faces held a peculiar kind of feral joy. The kind of insanity you might see in the eyes of a drunken prostitute at the end of a particularly rewarding evening.

A fat lady pushed him aside. By some piece of fortune he was shoved against a large unsightly plant pot. It was next to a small pedestal where he could sit for a second or two and catch his breath. Bailey reached in his pocket to pull his out his baccy tin as the raucous sound of an insane Santa automaton coursed like a twenty-one gun salute through his brain. The jolly red figure had emerged with all the subtlety of a cartoon Dracula from a coffin-shaped box on the arcade balcony. With shaking hands Bailey searched for his papers buried somewhere in his raincoat.

"You can't smoke here." It was a security guard. His neat uniform contrasted with a wan, wrinkled effort of a face.

"I wasn't going to smoke," said Bailey sourly. "I'm only rolling up."

The guard shrugged. "Smoking is not allowed."

Was the guard deaf? Some banal Christmas tune was telling him about snow.

"Only rolling up, not smoking …"

The guard shook his head. Bailey gave up. The interminable noise, the deaf guard. He put the baccy tin away and spilled half the contents in the process. The guard gave him a look. Bailey shrugged and bent over; his dodgy knee pained him but he managed to scrape up the baccy. For a second he thought about placing it back in the tin but the guard eyed him with a stony look and he was morally forced to stand and find a bin.

"Damn," he said under his breath. He felt like a criminal. Whatever happened to Christmas cheer? He surged across the moving crowd. Finally he found a bin full of fast food containers, boxes and plastic wrapping. With some regret he tipped the wad of tobacco into it. What a waste. His head beat with toxins. That extra pint in the bar at the station had kicked in.

Some kids were on their mobile phones next to the bin. It reminded Bailey that he had one somewhere. His wife insisted he take it as though he might get lost. He dug around in his pocket, retrieved the mobile phone and spent five minutes fiddling with the tiny buttons. Eventually, he found the house number.

"It's me," he said and attempted to inject some enthusiasm into his voice. "I'm at the Mall. That note slipped out of my hand ..."

Deirdre sounded far away. "God, can't you even keep a simple note?"

"I know where I'm going. Just wanted to check—"

"It's down stairs; the shop next to the CD store, James, between the pizza booth and the massage chairs. Where are you?"

Bailey didn't know. The whole place was just one swirling mass of bodies and bright lights. "I can see it," he said gruffly.

"Good, it's for the kids for Christ's sake, James. Get a grip. Have you been to the pub?"

"Of course not; came here directly. I was getting something for you."

There was silence. Did that mean the lie had worked? It was only a white lie. He had needed a drink. Was that the shop she meant, just ahead beyond the plastic tree?

"You've not lost my credit card have you?"

Bailey fingered his pockets and felt the clammy touch of leather.

"Of course not, love."

"Well hurry up or your tea will be in the dog."

The line went dead. Why had he bothered? He fingered his pockets again to ensure that his wallet was still there. Teenagers today, you never knew. Bailey thought he had just enough left for the present and a choice of a two way bet on the derby at New Year – which he would miss of course – or another quickie on the way home. It was no choice really. Deirdre would smell the beer if he had a pint before he caught the train. It couldn't be the shop she meant. It was somewhere downstairs. He remembered that at least.

A couple of young girls advanced towards him carrying immense bags of stuff. All these young things looked much the same; too much makeup, too few clothes. Mind you, in his day ... But it wasn't his day any more. He almost had to leap to avoid them. At some point between the age of twenty-seven and thirty-five he had become invisible to the opposite sex, a condition exacerbated by the festive season where every woman seemed to have become a kind of unseemly predator.

Where was that shop? Bailey searched for the elevator going down: fought his way past a mother and three kids after waiting for the third time. The elevator was crammed with sweating bodies. He became intensely aware that he stank. Or was it him? All the people on the lift looked ugly as sin, like dressed up dolls. There was something unnaturally unpleasant about them. Perhaps they were decent people if they didn't inhabit the Mall.

As the lift sunk into the depths he observed through its glass walls the crowds of shoppers sway and heave across the glittering floor like some vampiric ballet. The boutique mannequins lent a kind of caldarium voyeurism to their contortions as though they were silent observers of something sinful and naked. Synthetic Christmas music blared in Bailey's ears from the hidden lift speakers and for one surreal movement the occupants looked like they danced to its banal beat. It was a scene from Hieronymus Bosch, a depiction of endless torment.

Bailey shook his head. They descended another floor. Did this shopping centre have four floors? He'd never taken much of an interest in the place even though Deirdre seemed to have a second home in it somewhere. He felt thirsty and sick. The claustrophobia induced by the enclosed space, the terrible smell of sweat and a deeper visceral stench as though someone had released their bowels on the lift. Who would notice in this press? There was a jolt and, like a monster disgorging its cannibal breakfast, the occupants spilled into the arcade. As he tripped forward, kneed by the man behind him, Bailey noticed that this was the lowest floor. He had a vague memory that Deirdre had mentioned it as being his destination.

Bailey gave a whimper of relief. The crowds were not so thick here. The lights were fractionally dimmer and, God be thanked, there was a small bench. He pushed forward only to be thrust aside by a couple of youths sharing headphones in their ears. They stood, one foot on the bench, tapping their fingers. Bailey stared at their ghostly, spotted faces. If he had been a few years younger, if they could listen he would … And then, as suddenly as they had arrived, they left. The bench was empty. Bailey fell on it, banging his knee. He dropped his bag. Someone stepped on it. Somehow he clung on and then for a brief moment he was almost but not quite alone.

Bailey sat down heavily, pulled out his baccy tin then put it away with a sigh of regret. He'd need to wait until he escaped the Mall. He paused, weighing up his miserable life.

Deirdre wanted a divorce. He was pretty certain of that. The rot had started when she had ditched the cleaner's job at Bellport High. She'd fallen in with one of the English teachers there, Miss Calder; the ridiculous woman with blue hair who thought she was trendy and let the kids call her 'Julie'. Complete arsehole as far as Bailey was concerned. More like a schoolkid than the kids. Anyway, Deirdre had been impressed. Sometimes Bailey thought there might be some darker reason; an illicit lesbian affair or the like – now, what with the television and the computer, women got ideas. If only he hadn't lost his job. Perhaps it would be different. There had been no point in Deirdre earning peanuts with him on the dole. He kept trying, of course. Nothing came up. Deirdre started that yoga, and then there was the feng shui class – He couldn't even pronounce it. After that it was all downhill. She laughed at him; called him conservative and boring, told him some unpleasant things.

The final straw had been the coven – Deirdre called it her 'ladies group' but it was just witchcraft to Bailey. She knew his religious bent. Although he wasn't a Christian as such, the local church had been about the only thing that had kept him going through their relationship problems. Bailey supposed he was some sort of pantheist. He had a vague practical faith in God; that things would work out: sinners punished, the decent people saved. Sure, he had the odd drink and he liked to put

19

one on the horses but he was basically a moral person and some childhood lingerings of faith made him repent indiscretions.

Deirdre and her bloody coven; a stupid middle-class bunch of women who thought they could play at white magic. She called it invigorating; talked about spiritual release, dream catchers and chakras and God knows what else. A load of nonsense and if she wasn't careful these things could become dangerous. He'd heard stories about that. A job. That might sort it out. A bit of money, a holiday for her and the kids. A proper Christmas with a real tree and a good turkey dinner before the midnight service instead of this plastic crap and that awful muzak.

People drifted by, walking with slow uncertain steps as though lost. Christ. It was like the film, *Dawn of the Dead*. If you looked out of the corner of your eye it was quite scary. Bailey felt a peculiar unease. Then an elderly man joined him. For a second he resented the intrusion; then he realised that he might have found a kindred spirit.

"Bloody Christmas," he said as an opener. The man didn't reply. He sat in abject silence at Bailey's side. There was an awful smell, like something rotten. Bailey turned. The man was a complete mess, some sort of tramp. Bailey was surprised security hadn't turfed him out. He gave a quick glance and his stomach heaved. Christ, his face had rotted away at the cheek. Some kind of disease. Quickly Bailey got to his feet. He took another sidelong look at the tramp. The man sat in his withered grey mackintosh like a scarecrow. He was blind, or at least his eyes were glazed almost as though he had recently died. Was he breathing? For a second Bailey considered checking but that would take the biscuit. Let some other bugger ruin his Christmas. It was almost down the pan already. He lurched across the shiny floor and looked only at the feet plodding around him. He realised that he hated this place more than anything he could think of; perhaps even more than his wife.

Bailey shielded his eyes under the flickering lights. It was less bright here but bright enough with a green fluorescent glare that battered the senses. But in front of him he saw a pizza booth and there were some massage chairs with two old biddies getting mauled by an invisible robot. You only needed an ancient Durand Durand on the keyboard and it would be like *Barbarella* for coffin dodgers.

Bailey fingered the wallet in his pocket as he walked towards the chairs. Just beyond the old dears in the hazy light, he could see a small toyshop – franchise they called them in the ugly new world. Doubtless it was full of ginseng and Hopi ear candles or some new wave rubbish that Deirdre's group had discovered. He'd be surprised if it lasted long after Christmas what with the rates and the consumer's general preferences for throwaway crap.

As he moved towards the toyshop he stopped in amazement.

Beyond the massage chairs in a solitary corner was a bookshop; not a multinational concern or a chain store but a real second-hand bookshop. He advanced towards it, at every moment thinking that it might disappear. What the hell was it doing in this atrocity of a place? The lights were on: not flashing signs beneath an open fronted auditorium but dim lights, an honest door and a conventional sign: 'Book Emporium'; beneath it another handwritten missive: 'second-hand books bought and sold.'

Bailey stood before the window and felt the sweat of the collector run down his brow.

He'd loved books always; collected them since he'd got his first money on the paper round long, long ago. As an adult he'd never given up the bug until his courtship with Deirdre. At first she'd feigned interest but then she got more derisory as the kids grew up and their love grew cold. It had become a running battle over his stacks of genre fiction; one he had finally lost. The books and magazines were now confined to the attic. But whenever she was out at her ladies group, and the kids were safely in bed, he would sit amongst his precious books and sort them out; cataloguing, with an almost

21

pornographic lust, the few purchases he managed to sneak through the door.

And here, in the shop window, titles that sent a thrill through the heart stood in neat military rows. Bailey touched the window in disbelief. Amidst the usual mediocrity he saw the spines of NEL, Pan, Foursquare, Fontana. My God. Just beneath a tiny plastic Christmas tree a rack of vintage magazines lay in disarray: *Uncanny*, *Beyond* – numbers 1 and 2, *Startling Stories*, *Thrilling Mysteries*, and just under the main display in the front bookshelf were some Gollancz hardbacks, divided into Fantasy and SF. He peered a little closer, keen eyes inspecting titles and prices. The show pieces at the front – coffee-table books, romance and children's fairy tales were reasonably priced; he could see a bin at the side with a '50p' tag on it: unbelievable.

Bailey drew back from the window. The ridiculous song about snow was on again but he hardly heard it. How on earth had this shop ended up here? It certainly wouldn't be around in a year. It shouldn't be here at all. It should be in some back street next to the junk shops and the florists.

Bailey felt the clammy leather of his wallet. He had a couple of quid but Deirdre's credit card now burnt a hole in his pocket. She'd given him the card so that he could use it in the toyshop but he thought he could remember the pin number. He straightened up and with considerable reluctance drew away from the Aladdin's cave before him. The only thing that kept him from an immediate assault was the certain knowledge that no one in this grotesque Mall would be remotely interested in the shop. The consumers were out for shiny new toys, PCs, mobile phones and things that he couldn't even name.

A crowd of aimless people blocked his way. They all had their backs to him as they watched a screen display in the open front of some new flat screen franchise. They were showing some sickly Santa film, a new production with actors that looked about twelve years old. Even with the sound off, it was unbearable. The two old dears were still in the massage chairs.

From behind they looked like twin Frankenstein brides about to resurrect.

Bailey squeezed through the crowd to the lift. His throat was dry. He'd almost forgotten about a smoke in the excitement. The lift was empty but he had no idea where the cash machine was located. He'd have to ask at the information desk he'd seen on the way in. Or maybe it would be on one of those great shields he'd passed by the escalators. Would he have time for a cigarette? The thought of these books was enough to dismiss the idea.

It took him an eternity to find a cash machine – in the process he lost all sense of direction and never even got near the information desk. The shields with their lists of shops and complex maps had been utterly bewildering. But luckily on the third floor a machine seemed to appear out of nowhere.

Bailey waited in a short queue nervously toying with Deirdre's card. He was in a kind of daze. Every moment seemed wasted. He kept thinking about his kids and Deirdre waiting at home. Explanations about his need for the cash, played over his tongue and increasingly fantastic lies ran through the labyrinth of his mind. Eventually he got to the front of the queue. He made two attempts at cash withdrawal but was dismayed to find he'd lost the sequence of the pin. Some middle-aged bloke began mouthing at him in a strange guttural voice and he couldn't take the risk of losing the card. Dismally, he left the queue.

For a few seconds he held the card in his sweating hand and then he found a space against a wall between a boutique and a hairdresser. People kept brushing past him in their haste and the snow still fell in that sickly Christmas song. He leaned against the wall. Somehow he got the mobile phone out his pocket and after a frantic duel with the buttons he found the house number. Busy! Bailey cursed inwardly. He tried again. Deirdre's clipped accent was barely audible above the music and a sustained burst of Santa laughter.

"What the hell is it, James? The kids are just out of the bath.

I thought you'd be home by now."

"Sorry, love," the lie had shrunk to something manageable. "I tried to get you a little thing but I ..." his mind raced with amounts and book covers, "... I'm short of fifteen quid."

Deirdre took on a suspicious tone. "You're not just going to the pub?"

"Of course not, love. It's Christmas Eve. I can't wait to get home ... the kids."

"Well." Her voice seemed to relax. "Why not use my card."

It was more than he'd hoped for. "That's brilliant. I don't have the number."

There was a brief hesitation then Deirdre passed on the pin number.

"Is it something nice?" she said coquettishly.

"Secret," Bailey replied.

She cackled and put down the phone. Just before it disengaged he heard Tommy and Sara shout from the bathroom. He felt a momentary guilt. Fortunately he had a present for Deirdre – bra and knickers he'd got from a friend at the old workshop. The set looked to be worth about thirty quid. The difficulty would be to get the books home. Then he smiled. It would be easy. If he had the books wrapped he could pretend they were the present, sneak them up to the attic and swap.

Some lout banged into him with a bag but he almost smiled. Bloody Christmas! The glaring lights were still awful, the music was worse; his head beat with toxins, he was now hungry and he wanted a smoke but Bailey felt a warm glow enervate his insides. He waited another ten minutes in the queue for the cash machine and got twenty quid out. With a strut in his step he weaved through the masses.

When he got back to the lift it was temporarily out of order. After a moment in which the whole crowd milled round like a human whirlpool he followed a security guard to the escalator. Jostled and shoved, he got down to the first floor to find the lift working again. Three times it went up and down and on the third he pressed in with a bunch of ugly looking schoolchildren.

As they went down again he smelled a rank foetid smell. He glanced at the children. Were they mentally impaired? Had one of them filled his pants? The children seemed about ages with his Sara. But there were no accompanying adults. Bailey felt a sudden lurch of anxiety. Had the adults been left on the other floor? The lift doors opened. Bugger them, he thought. A security guard can sort it out. The children wandered out of the lift without any apparent purpose. Three of them just stood in his way like aimless animals. After a moment's hesitation he somewhat roughly pushed them aside.

The light was dimmer again. The old tramp was still on the bench but seemed to have moved, or perhaps slumped would be a better word. The children shouldn't see that, Bailey thought. Then he shook his head in disgust. He had little enough time as it was. The crowd still watched the same turgid film and two old ladies were at the massage chairs again – or were they the same ones? Bailey had no idea. He paused for a second. Should he get the present from the toyshop or go directly to the bookshop? He knew himself well enough by now to realise that he could lose himself in a good bookshop so the sensible thing would be to secure the present Deirdre was after. But the money was burning holes in his pockets. He rounded the last few people seeing only legs and feet.

Bailey looked up. In a moment of torment he thought the bookshop had gone – as though he had imagined it all. The shop light seemed dimmer. He advanced to the window. It *was* dimmer. In the shadows he could see someone sitting at a desk. Christ. The shop was shut! He felt a flutter in his heart then he saw a small hand written sign. '*Back in ten minutes.*'

Bailey sighed with relief. It wasn't so bad. He could get this toyshop out of the way and with a bit of luck the proprietor would be open for business again by the time he had finished. He glanced at the toyshop next door but saw nothing. His eyes were inexorably drawn to the display in the bookshop. He was a fish on a hook, an iron filing on a magnet. Like a child at a sweetshop, he began to eat the sweets before they were in his mouth.

Bailey had covered the whole gamut of the shop window in about fifteen seconds and had marked down at least one definite and three probables. He moved to the glass-fronted door where he could see a couple of bargain boxes on the floor at twenty pence a go.

If his heart had fluttered before it nearly stopped at that moment. He crouched to his knees, eyes widened in awe.

Bailey had only seen pictures of it in collectors magazines but he had heard about it often enough.

The dust jacket was intact, perfect condition as far as he could see, but when it had been thrown on the box the jacket had half slipped off to reveal the grey boards beneath. The lewdly open page bore the legend, *Tales of the Grotesque: A collection of uneasy tales – L. A. Lewis.*

Even in the uncertain light, Bailey could pick out the signature of the author. Apart from being a thing of beauty in itself, Bailey knew it was worth over two thousand smackers.

And it was sitting in the twenty pence box. The proprietor – who was still at his desk – obviously had no idea. Bailey smirked inwardly. There couldn't be a living soul within the Mall who would know it. He pondered whether just to knock on the window but it didn't seem right. Booksellers could be reclusive types. He gawped at the book for a few more moments. Should he knock? Christ, he needed a smoke bad now. He shook himself and tried to be rational. He could nip next door, get the present and if the proprietor of the bookshop still hadn't opened maybe he could just prompt him a bit. Certainly he could wait at the door until the bloke felt embarrassed enough to open.

Caught in two minds, Bailey stood for a little longer, surveying the book like a visitant lover. He was reassured because in the short time that he looked nobody even came near. Then the reassurance broke down like cracking ice. He visualised the book slipping out of his grasp into the hands of some chance collector or worse one of the idiots in the Mall who'd use it as a bookend or write his grocery list on the cover. Just for one awful second, in the reflections in the window he saw the massed crowds behind him. They were all dead: walking corpses, cadaverous faces with rotted limbs projecting from ragged graveclothes. Instinctively, Bailey turned and pressed his back to the shop window. As he turned, he raised his hands to his face in futile defence to look through the prison of his fingers like a child at peek-a-boo.

Of course, all was as before. The masses still watched the flat screen, the geriatrics lolled in the massage chairs, the tramp slumped on the distant bench. The lost children were now pressed against a shop window. The crowds of the Mall still milled around like zombies but were obviously not really dead – unless the tramp was dead but he wasn't walking. Bailey shrugged it off. He needed a smoke badly and a pint would come in useful. The nicotine and alcohol withdrawal could sometimes lighten the blood and make him dizzy. He scratched the stubble on his chin. The book was safe enough for a few minutes. Best get the present Deirdre was after. A little shamefacedly he pushed himself from the bookshop window.

Deirdre had said he only needed to pick up a preordered package. An old woman and a teenager stood like mannequins outside the toyshop. They stared into infinity, clutching fast food. Bailey felt the faint pangs of hunger dissolve as he walked towards the shop. What were they making in the pizza booth? Bailey had a vague impression of its confines crammed with teenagers who wolfed down their meals from boxes. But it stank to high heaven. It could even be the source of the smell, some failure of the air conditioning. Bailey rushed past, and with a grimace, opened the toyshop door. He was relieved to find that inside, the smell was suppressed by some sort of incense.

The toyshop was much as he expected given Deirdre's new

fad. Awful wooden toys, massage oils and expensive herbal teas, hand knitted jumpers and socks. In short, all the overpriced stuff that no child would enjoy and no sensible adult would buy; all borne out by the absence of customers.

Behind a glittering shambles of gemstones, joss sticks and Chinese balls, which shrouded a broad wooden desk was an elfin-like woman. Bailey wanted to get the business done as quickly as possible but it was the sort of shop where you had to appear interested in all the crap and potter around. He couldn't be bothered. He approached the counter and blurted out:

"My wife is expecting a package. I have to pick it up."

The woman stared at him mirthlessly. She was some sort of dwarf, a congenital condition perhaps.

"Package?"

"Yes, a present for the kids. The name is Bailey." He vaguely recognised the woman's idiotic face. Doubtless she was one of Deirdre's new friends.

"Package," she said in a voice bereft of tone. Christ, it was Christmas. What did she expect?

"Bailey?"

"Deirdre Bailey," he said bursting with impatience.

"Sorry," she said. "I'm not sure I have any package to be collected."

"One minute," Bailey replied. He drew out his mobile phone.

"Sorry," said the woman. "We don't allow phones in the shop." She pointed to a list of commandments on the wall.

Bailey resisted the temptation to scowl, indicated the phone and walked back outside into the stinking Mall. He tried the house again. The phone rang for some time. He thought he'd connected and began to say that the package wasn't there but the phone cut off. Trying again he found it was dead. "Jesus," he moaned, glancing across to the bookshop. The lights were on. Even from the distance he could see that the '*back in ten minutes*' sign was still up.

With a growing desperation he went back to the toyshop.

The woman was gone from the counter but he could see a rear section of the shop that he'd missed the first time. Inside the oblong room, he found to his surprise that the shelves were full of automata, German and Swiss mechanical toys, dioramas houses and weird moving figures. The woman was on a step winding up a clockwork doll's house. On another day he might have had a decent look. The toys were quite something.

"Excuse me," he said to the woman's back. "I can't get through to my wife." He waited an interminable time as she struggled down from the step and turned towards him. She looked like a mechanical toy herself, something you might find in one of the Grimm's fairy tales.

"What was the name again?"

"Bailey, Deirdre Bailey."

"I'll just check; we sometimes leave packages behind the alchemy counter."

Alchemy counter? Oh, God, thought Bailey. Alchemy! If I don't get a cigarette I'm going to kill someone. He followed her to a back counter stacked with labelled bottles and boxes. She pottered around behind it.

In an attempt to keep himself occupied, Bailey made to touch one of the bottles.

"Please," she said quickly. "Don't touch those. Some are quite dangerous. Those small green bottles contain ground rosary pea. Eat even a little and you would die." The woman stooped under the counter still searching. Typical, thought Bailey. There's probably a law against it but these people are all the same; make their own rules. He really hated them, probably as much as he now hated Deirdre and what she had become.

And then Bailey enjoyed a sudden madness. Perhaps he had subconsciously begun the chain of action when his inner voice had whispered the word 'kill'. However the impulse had come about, his actions superseded any conscious volition. With a quick movement he stealthily slipped a green bottle into his pocket. There were so many bottles and potions it would never

29

be missed.

Bailey did not intend to kill his wife. It was difficult to express the feeling in any concrete terms. Perhaps it was simply that he now had a bottle of deadly poison in his pocket. Somehow it gave him a kind of internal edge, a pressure valve; as though the very possession of the bottle prevented him from doing anything silly.

The dwarf lady peeked over the counter. Bailey assumed a holier than thou expression.

"I've just remembered," she said with an idiotic smirk. "Mrs Bailey picked up the package this morning."

"But that can't be," said Bailey. "She sent me specifically to get it."

"Yes, she did," said the lady. "But she has it already."

Bailey was past argument. His chest hurt and his head spun. All his thoughts rested on the floor of the bookshop next door, where, in the twenty pence box, lay a first edition of *Tales of the Grotesque* written by L. A. Lewis; a book that sported a priceless signature and looked like Heaven. Even just to hold that wondrous thing for a few minutes would be an experience and, should he decide to sell it later on, he'd be sitting on thousands. Deirdre could stuff it. He'd had enough. He stared with impassive dignity at the tiny woman before him. "Forget it," he said. She looked at him with a disturbing smile as he walked back into the Mall.

The smell hit him, the stifling heat and the glaring lights. More crowds had gathered like sediment at the bottom of a septic tank. People shuffled by. He looked for a clock to check the time, but of course these places never had them. Fortunately, the bookshop doorway was still free. These animals wouldn't know a book if it whacked them on the head. Quickly he thrust towards the door. The '*back in ten minutes*' sign had gone. Bailey could see the proprietor sat at his desk. With the satisfied smile of a man coming home, Bailey pushed the door.

It was locked.

Bailey checked again. There were no closing times; only 'Book Emporium' and the bookshop legend 'second-hand books bought and sold.' above the door. He waved at the man but there was no response. He knocked on the window. The man did not move. Bailey knocked again. Christ, the proprietor must be asleep. He tired knocking again. Nothing. Breathing heavily he rested against the door and tried to think.

The shops would surely close soon. At the worst he could wait at the door with the cash in his hand. He'd definitely catch him on the way out. In the meantime a quick smoke and he'd dash back. He must have at least an hour or so before the proprietor packed up.

Bailey cursed to himself and turned to face the Mall.

A security guard stood on guard at the escalator, the conductor of a crowd that had grown in size and scope so that it resembled nothing less than the *exquisite corpse* of a surrealist parlour game. Predatory consumers lurched and heaved across its glittering halls like rival regiments of reanimated cadavers. The heat was stifling and the stench horrendous. Somewhere, hidden speakers blared out the banal song about snow but their volume had increased and the Santa automaton seemed to have developed a fault; its insane laughter sent a distorted cadence of ululation across the arcade.

In the distance, Bailey saw the huge shield that advertised directions. Its proclamations appeared, to his despairing eyes, more complex than the worst trigonometry exam. After a short struggle behind a crowd of middle-aged women, he pressed on through a horde of lost children, past a solitary guard and a gang of vacuous teenagers, to finally make a stand beneath its monolithic shadow. He stared upwards with baffled eyes at signs and logos for shops he had never heard of that sold things he didn't want for desires he didn't possess or need and pretensions he didn't have. There were signs for toilets, lifts, escalators and changing rooms. There was an arrow to the information desk and emblems for the first aid area, the prayer room and Santa's grotto but amidst the bewildering variety of signs, arrows, emblems and logos there were none that actually indicated an exit.

*

Deirdre had saved the big box for last. The children sat amidst the Christmas paper and the discarded boxes. Shining toys lay scattered on the carpet. They both knew this was the one.

"Shall we leave it until after Christmas dinner," she teased.

"No," said Tommy. He was younger and hadn't quite mastered deferred gratification.

"Mummy," said Sara. "Where's daddy?"

Deirdre had been waiting for her to latch on. "Well," she said carefully, "I'm afraid Daddy has gone. But never mind. We'll get along just fine, the three of us."

Sara nodded.

"Can I open it?" said Tommy. At five years of age, practical difficulties were more immediate than abstract possibilities.

"Let mummy," said Deirdre. "It's a bit delicate."

Carefully, she unwrapped the box.

"Ooooh," said Sara. Tommy stood up.

In the box was something that looked like a large toy house.

"It's for girls," said Tommy with some disappointment.

Sara drew closer. "It's not a doll's house, silly. It's a shopping mall."

Tommy drew closer, reluctantly. He peered in at the windows. "There's little people in there, moving about," he said with a faint unease.

"Yes," said Deirdre. "I made it at my ladies group."

"I don't like it," said Tommy with finality. "I think we should throw it on the fire."

"Not yet," said Deirdre under her breath.

SALVAJE

Simon Bestwick

I woke up and didn't know why; it happened, since I fell pregnant, especially as I got nearer to term, my belly bigger and the child more restless. But this time felt different.

You know when a noise in a dream starts you awake, and you can't be sure whether it was a real one or not? It was like that. Beside me, Jim let out a snore. He could sleep through anything; I envied that, sometimes till I felt like hitting him.

Then the stairs creaked, and I knew it wasn't the baby that'd woken me up.

"Jim." I hissed it, grabbing his arm, but was already fumbling on the bedside table. I gripped and shook him, turned on the light. He grunted, and the door flew open.

"Don't move!" It was whispered, but might as well have been shouted. The man wore a balaclava hood and carried a gun. A pistol, it was silenced. He was aiming it at my face. "Don't move, you fucking bitch, don't you fucking move."

Two others came into the room, masked and holding guns as well. A third followed, smaller and thinner – a girl or a younger man, a boy even. He or she held a knife.

The upstairs phone was inches from my hand. The silencer jerked sideways, twice; I got the message and pulled my hand away. "Frank, get the phone," the gunman said. The boss, he must be.

Frank – I assumed it was him, he was the one who moved – grabbed the phone and pulled it clear, tearing the cord loose of the wall. He made sure he never strayed between the big man's gun and me.

The third gunman came round the bed, aiming at Jim. "Don't fucking move, don't – fucking – move."

Jim raised his hands into plain view. "What do you want?"

The gunman lunged forward, hitting him in the face with the butt of the gun. "Shut your fucking face, you cunt, just shut it."

"Tyler," said the boss man. Tyler stepped back. Jim let out a moan. "Shut up," the boss man said. "Use the sheets to catch the blood."

There was no kindness in that last – it was matter-of-fact, offhand. He had a job to do and wanted to get on with it. I could see their eyes and there was nothing in them, no pity or kindness at all. Tyler's eyes looked as if he might be smiling. The boss's eyes were just empty, like a fish on a slab. I could hear Jim's breathing, painful and muffled, and another set of breaths – the boy, excited.

I had no idea who these men were, but I recognised them all the same. Grandpa would've too; it was thanks to them I knew their kind. *Franquistas*, he'd've called them, and like as not spat hard at the fireplace, which always used to drive my mother mad. It wasn't just the men he'd fought in his youth; I'd heard it spat out as a little girl, when footage of the Miners' Strike was on and we saw the police beating the strikers with their batons. I was too young to understand, but I did now. Pinochet in Chile, too, the Americans in Iraq; they were *Franquistas* all – different names and countries, but the same breed.

Seconds passed, almost a minute the boss was letting things cool. There was a job to do. I knew what it must be, the only thing it could be. "You," he told me, "get out of bed."

Jim made a muffled noise of protest and reached for me. Tyler lunged forward and hit him again; this time the boss said nothing.

I got out of bed, slowly and carefully because the child made me unsteady. I wore a nightdress, so I wasn't naked in front of them, but I had nothing on underneath and the material wasn't thick – it was only early autumn and we had central heating. The boy was staring at my breasts and I covered them, moved my hand over my belly. I hesitated between covering my pubis and trying to shield my unborn, somehow.

*

My grandfather's name was Tomas Bardillo. He was from Spain, as you may've guessed. If you have, you probably guessed he fought in the Civil War, on the side of the Republic. He was at Teruel and Boadilla, and later, after the fall of Madrid, when Franco and the Falangists ruled Spain, he fought almost six years with the partisans in the mountains. According to Grandpa, many of them thought when the Allies invaded Europe, they'd come to get rid of all the Fascists – not just Hitler and Mussolini, but Franco in Spain and Salazar in Portugal too, even though neither had taken sides in the Second World War. When that didn't happen, my grandfather was one of many who lost heart. He crossed the border into France in 1946, one step ahead of Falangists who wanted to hunt him down and kill him.

He stayed in France almost a year, and then he met my grandmother, an English nurse. I don't know what made him move to England; in many ways he felt betrayed by the British, who'd turned a blind eye to the Civil War when it was on and who'd been content to leave Franco in power now. Then again, he always spoke well of British lads from the International Brigades that he'd fought with, so maybe that was it.

He only went back to Spain once, in the seventies after Franco died, to pay his respects, look for old comrades. I don't know what he found because he never spoke about that, not even to me, and I was his favourite. But he never went back again.

*

They didn't let me put on a dressing gown or slippers, not even when it was time to leave the house. It was how they kept me vulnerable. Poor Jim must've felt worse; he always slept naked.

The boss man was called Blackthorn; he rolled up his balaclava hood to show a round face with a moustache and buzz-cut hair. Ex-army, I reckoned. A mercenary, perhaps, or just in need of a job, any job.

"Do you know why we're here?" he asked me.

I looked at him and said nothing.

Blackthorn sighed. "I'll make this simple for you, darling. When I ask a question I want it answered. When you answer it you answer me straight – you tell me the truth and you don't try to trick me. If you break any of those rules your husband gets shot. Shoulders, knees. And so on. And if you keep fannying us about, love, then Max over there," – Max was the boy with the knife – "slits your hubby's throat ear to fucking ear. Have you got that or do you want me to go over it again?"

"I've got it," I said.

"So?"

I nodded. "I know why you're here."

"Good. Where's what we want?"

"It's not here."

Blackthorn breathed out through his nose.

"But I know where it is."

"Don't piss me around, cunt."

"It's in the hills," I said. "He buried it there."

"Where?"

"I'll take you."

"I know. Max?"

"Boss?" The boy's voice was breathy, edgy, eager.

Blackthorn nodded at Jim. "Tie this twat to the chair. If he gives you any shit, hurt him."

"Gotcha."

Blackthorn looked at me. "I've got me mobile. If you piss us about up there, it just takes one phone call. Max hasn't got a gun, but he can do a lot of damage with that knife of his. Right, Max?"

"Yeah." The breathy voice broke into a giggle. "I practice."

I wondered what on. Probably not people, not yet, not till now. Animals, most likely, but he'd love to move on to the next step.

"Do you understand?" Blackthorn asked.

"Yes," I said.

"Good girl. Be good and do as you're told and we'll be on our way and all you've got to do is wash the sheets and get hubby's conk looked at."

I didn't know whether to believe him. If they got what they wanted, it was a robbery – if they killed us, there'd be a murder hunt. But Blackthorn had let me see his face, and these men were professionals – I knew that for a fact. They were soldiers, most of them, or had been. They'd know how to cover their tracks. Dead witnesses were better than living ones. There was no knowing what'd happen when I led them to what they wanted.

I knew that in that case, I might never see Jim again. If they thought my cooperation was a foregone conclusion, they wouldn't need Jim alive. Max might well slit his throat as soon as we were gone and make ready to leave with the rest when they got back. There was nothing I could do about that; my one chance against them would be on the hill. I was a woman, a civilian, and I was pregnant; they would underestimate me for that. That might give me a chance, but it might also rob Jim of one.

I moved towards him, but Tyler grabbed my arm roughly and pulled me back. "Get fucking moving."

We said goodbye to each other without words. He was terrified. I couldn't blame him. Jim had many virtues – he was kind, gentle, bright, witty, a good cook, a good husband, would make a good father – but a fighter, he wasn't.

I didn't look back as they led me down the hall. In the time I had – to walk barefoot down the damp, freezing cold drive, to travel through the Lancashire town where we lived in the small morning hours and up into the hills – in those minutes, I must do a difficult thing, and accept my husband as dead in my heart. I must also shut my ears to the pain that cried from me at that knowledge, must tell that voice to be silent, that mourning and grief must wait till later. I knew that I could do it. Jim was not a fighter, but I was. And now I was at war.

*

In many ways Jim was like my father. I think Dad disappointed Grandpa because he wasn't a fighter, didn't have that spirit. He was a good man, though, and that's why I loved him.

Grandpa, though – well, what a Grandpa. I was a bit of a tomboy, as a girl – I asked him what he'd done in the war, and that was how I learned about Spain. Much to my Mum's disapproval. She was never that keen on Grandpa.

He liked her, though, because she had the spirit my father didn't. Whenever she blew up over something, Grandpa'd smile. He wasn't mocking her; it was admiration, although I don't know if she realised that. He could see her in me, and something of himself too.

"You're a fighter, Luisa," he used to say. "A fighter, heh?"

"Yes, Grandpa."

Mum thought he mocked her, thought he encouraged me to be a tomboy. I loved them all, though, even if they fought among themselves. Family. I had a good one, I suppose.

But of all of them, it was Grandpa who taught me most. Later on in life, when I was in my teens and early twenties and his health had begun to fail, I'd visit him and we'd talk, more seriously, as adults.

"Never believe it cannot happen to you, Luisa," I remember him telling me. "Never believe that you are safe from the *Franquistas*. All countries have such men. They only need their chance. And if it comes – well, you may have to fight. Only if you must, but such men often leave you with no choice."

And he would tell me things that I needed to know. How there was always a choice – to panic, to let fear or grief or pain rule, or to step back, give it its place, but keep control, look for what could be done, and what must be.

"It is not easy," he said. "Not the learning to act like this, but the doing. What must be done."

He wasn't looking at me when he said that. He was remembering things – maybe some things that he never told me at all, because there are always things in a life too dark and painful to share. Or too shameful.

*

But that was how I could ride in a car with killers, knowing my husband might be dead, knowing I might be to die, but not panic, fight for control, and plan my war.

The dark was thinning to a dull greyness over the land; artificial lights burned through it like candles or embers. Mostly it was only the streetlights of the town, or now and again, another pair of far-off headlamps. Otherwise, the town looked grey and dead. The hills were being unveiled in the distance, their green showing through as the car climbed the road. Then we entered the woodlands and the trees closed around us.

I looked straight ahead. Tyler drove. Blackthorn and Frank sat in the back of the car. Now and again, the muzzle of a silenced gun would brush through my hair and plant a cold kiss behind my ear or on the back of my neck; it was the intimacy of rapists.

Franquistas, I thought, and prayed for the strength to kill them if I could find the chance.

"Which way now?" Blackthorn said at last.

"Just keep going, straight ahead, for now."

He breathed out through his nose again.

"It's easier if I show you," I said. "It's just straight on for a while."

"Just don't piss about, bitch, alright?"

"I won't." I knew I sounded too calm. I should sound more frightened. Or perhaps they thought I was numb with shock.

"Can I ask something?" I said at last.

"No you fucking can't," said Tyler, "so just shut your

fucking trap, alright?"

I stayed silent. The car moved on through unending archways of trees. Now and then, Tyler would flash the headlights at a bend, and through a break in the tree cover I could see a farmer's field and beyond it the town, more hills, the distant cluster of another town in the distance.

Eventually Blackthorn spoke. "What?"

"What?"

"What did you want to ask?"

"I just …" I shrugged. "I wondered who hired you."

A silencer jabbed hard into the back of my head. "Mind your fucking own," said Frank.

I couldn't see the look Blackthorn gave him, but a look there must have been because Frank mumbled an apology – to his boss, not me. "Does it matter?" Blackthorn asked.

I shrugged.

"Someone in Spain. Who else? Your granddad took summat didn't belong to him. Someone's family wants it back."

Blackthorn didn't say any more. Maybe he didn't know any more than that. It was too much, anyway, and it told me I'd be killed. Jim was almost certainly dead.

Who was it? An old Falangist, most like, or a new one – someone's grandson, carrying on the tradition, not able to let anything go. But then, was I so different from that?

"They found something your granddad'd written. An old diary. It was enough. Something about salvage."

I tried not to smile.

"What's so fucking funny?" said Tyler. "Think this is fucking funny, do you, slag?"

"Her old granddad was a thief, wasn't he?" said Frank. "What's funny 'bout that?"

"He was a fucking Red an' all, wannee?" said Tyler.

"Fucking commies," said Frank. "Fucking Reds make me sick."

"Too fucking right," said Tyler. "Remember them carrying on when we was sorting the Micks out in Ulster. Or the Pakis in the Gulf."

You didn't get Pakistanis in Iraq, I wanted to say. But would there really be any point? They were *Franquistas*. Life was as simple and as complicated as that. There were two kinds of people in the world, ultimately – the *Franquistas* and their masters on the one side, and everyone else on the other. When it came down to it, there wasn't a middle ground, there couldn't be.

We were close to the top of the hill. To the right was a narrow dirt track, almost overgrown with brambles. "Down there," I said, as we passed it. Tyler cursed, jabbed me in the face with an elbow, and backed up before turning down it.

*

Grandpa died in 1997; he was in his eighties. He'd seemed indestructible till only a few years before, when the years of smoking began to catch up with him.

It was painful to watch; he dwindled away and was in constant pain, that or struggling to breathe, the workings of his lungs slow and tortured. I'd go to him, read him books – some in Spanish, which I struggled with – tell him about my life, or listen to his last few stories.

Some of them I'd heard before; some I hadn't. But, near the end, there was one story in particular. I remember it well.

It was autumn; I remember that. The trees were growing naked outside, the leaves dying slowly, turning the ground russet and gold. The light was failing; they and the streetlights coming on, cherry-red, outside the hospital, and the lights in the hospital buildings, were the only sources of colour and brightness.

I was reading him a poem by Cesar Vallejo, which he loved, usually, but his attention had wandered. It wasn't the pain, though, and nor was it memories – not in the usual sense that distracted him, when he retreated into his past, the lost battles, the lost friends and loves (my grandmother had died years before, when I was seven, a couple of days after my seventh birthday in point of fact). This time, it looked as if he was mulling something over, except that's too painless a word. There was something he was debating furiously with himself – whether he should share it or not.

At last, he let a short breath out through his nose and nodded to himself. I stopped reading.

He looked at me. "Put that book down, Luisa," he said, and I did. "There's something I need to tell you."

"Okay," I said.

He looked at me, hard. "Do you think I'm going mad, *bonita*?" He hadn't called me that in years.

"No." I was surprised he'd asked. At worst, he'd been less than lucid when the pain was bad, or right after they'd given him something for it.

"Good. Good. Because I must tell you something, and it is a strange story. You may find it hard to believe. But somebody must know, because …"

"Because?"

"Because the *Franquistas* are always with us, *bonita*; and they do not forget."

*

Proof of that, if it were needed: I stumbled along the dirt track, now, barefoot, in the half-light. It was mud and mire underfoot, but uneven, with sharp stones. My cheek was swelling up, bruised, from where Tyler had hit me, and I could taste blood in my mouth. I needed to pee, my feet hurt, and Blackthorn and the others kept pushing me from behind. I almost fell, twice.

"Move your fat arse, bitch," said Tyler, and my hatred grew. Soon I would not be able to contain or control it, I was afraid; that or my fear. I wanted to cry, but must not; we were almost there.

The clearing was almost in sight; one of them kicked me in

the backside and I fell. My control broke and I screamed in panic – *the baby, the baby.* I curled up as I fell, landed on my back with a cry of pain. My waters, my waters – no, they hadn't broken.

"Get up." Frank, looming over me. "I said get up!" He kicked at my stomach. I rolled, the boot glancing off my elbow. The toe of the boot caught the bone and the pain was awful.

"Get fucking up!" The boot, the boot—

"Alright!" I screamed it, scrambling away, struggling to a crouch. Tyler coming forward, pistol in my face – "Keep it fucking down!" He hissed it, warm spittle spattering my face.

I was still, crouching, covered in mud. "Shit yourself, darling?" one of them asked.

I managed to rise. *Oh, I will kill you; just give me that chance.*

"Where is it?" asked Blackthorn.

"Here. Over here." I moved forward, cradling my belly; I almost sobbed with relief as I felt the baby kick.

Calm, bonita. *Calm. You are almost there.*

Nettles and brambles caught my ankles. I gasped and whimpered from the pain. Finally I pointed at a patch of brambles.

"Stay there," said Blackthorn. Frank stood and pointed his gun at me, two-handed. He'd taken his hood off; they all had on the drive up. He had a moustache too; his face was flabby and low-browed, scars tracking through the thick black stubble on his head. Tyler moved past him with a shovel; he was the biggest one, head almost shaved bald – another moustache, brown hair, and almost no front teeth. His eyes were watery and grey. All the details sprang out, despite the dulling, leaden grey of the light. But through the trees, in the distance, I could see the first bright glimmer of true dawn.

Tyler set to with a vengeance, hacking and tearing at the earth. What he was looking for was a couple of feet down, through earth and roots, but it didn't take him long; the glimmer of dawn was no brighter when his shovel hit the metal box.

"Got it!" he said.

"Get it out."

"Not till after we're married, darling!" Tyler called, and he and Frank both cackled.

"Shut it!" barked Blackthorn. "Get the box up now."

"Do her now, boss?" Frank asked, raising the gun.

"Not yet," Blackthorn said. Frank hissed in disappointment, licking his lips. "Let's make sure first."

The box wasn't big, just one foot by two. Tyler dumped it on the ground and smashed off the padlock with his shovel. "Moment of truth," he said.

Blackthorn looked at me. "If you're fucking us about here, bitch, your hubby dies slowly."

Then Jim was alive. "I'm not," I said, not letting my hopes show.

Tyler opened the lid. He lifted out a heavy object, unwrapped it, frowned. "That's *it*?" he said.

It was a wolf's head, or a sculpture of one; it was made from a dull metal like pewter or lead. It was crudely done but somehow all the more convincing for it; the mouth snarled, teeth bared, and the eyes were more narrow and pitiless than even these men that I must kill.

Blackthorn shrugged. "What they paid us for," he said, and lifted his head to nod to Frank.

"Before you do it ..." I said, and they looked at me, and Blackthorn raised a hand. "Before you do, can I look? Please?" They stared. "I've never seen it," I said, lamely.

They exchanged glances. Tyler shrugged. Frank rolled his eyes and looked impatient to get on. "Alright," Blackthorn said. He had what he wanted and I'd done as I was told. He pointed to Frank. "She tries anything ..."

Frank nodded.

Tyler held the wolf's-head out to me. It snarled, lips rolled back from its teeth. I touched the cold metal, felt it burn my hands, like ice, and then I leant forward and kissed its mouth.

"What the fuck ..." Tyler spluttered in disgust, his last words to my knowledge, as I felt a cold breath leave the wolf's mouth and pass into mine.

*

In late 1944, the Allies were fighting their way across Occupied Europe, through the Low Countries and through France. The Russians were driving the Nazis back from the East. Caught between the two, Fascist Europe began to crack and crumble, except in Portugal and Spain.

In the mountains, the guerillas took heart, hoping aid would soon come; in Madrid, there was fear. Neither lasted as it eventually became plain that the Allies would not seek to topple Franco or Salazar. But in late '44, word reached Tomas Bardillo's guerilla group that a squad of elite Falangist troops were entering the mountain range – not to seek and destroy them, but in search of an object that might aid the Fascist war effort should the Allies invade.

What was unusual was its supposed nature; an artefact credited with supernatural powers. There was little enough belief in any of that among the mountaineers – they weren't religious, the Church being ranged solidly on the Falangist side. That said, the *Franquistas* weren't superstitious fools, so the decision was made to thwart the squad by any means necessary.

My grandfather was one of the party that set out to take them on. The battle in the mountains was fierce and bloody, both sides sustaining heavy losses, but ultimately the Fascist squad was wiped out, and the object they'd been seeking fell into the guerilla's hands.

So far, so good. But here was where my grandfather's account grew murky:

One of the guerillas got hold of the artefact – a wolf's head made of an unknown metal, and made use of it. That was what killed the Fascists; a man with a wolf's spirit or soul, immune to bullets, to any weapon that wasn't silver.

The guerilla used it again on several occasions, but ultimately it destroyed him. Each time, the wolf left its mark: by the end, he was little more than an animal, and killed himself in his last act as a thinking human being.

My grandfather had written some of his diary in Spanish, and some in English, in the hope of confusing the enemy if it fell into their hands. His j's, I remembered, had often been indistinguishable from his g's. He hadn't written *salvage* in his diary; he hadn't written in English at all. He'd written in Spanish: *salvaje*. Savage. Wild.

"It sounds like a child's tale, I know," my grandfather said, that autumn evening in the hospital as he lay dying. "But I saw it myself. The wolf's head has terrible power – real power. It can make a man invincible – but at such a cost, *bonita*, at such a cost ..." He lifted his head off the pillow. "But I tell you this because you need to know."

Yes, Grandpa.

Because the *Franquistas* are always with us. And they do not forget.

*

"You fucking bitch! You sick fucking twisted bitch!"

I know rage; do you? The threat to life – your own and those you love: your husband, your unborn child. The leering, grinning sadism of the enemy. The helplessness and the humiliation. All become a consuming rage, a willingness, a desire, finally a need, to tear flesh and to drink blood.

It sang in me; I embraced it and I loved it. Vengeance and vengeance, destruction and fury, pulling me ever on. Wanting to swallow me, whole, consume me; I would never be weak or helpless again, all I had to do was give into it, to—

No, no. I fought against it; it was sated, it had fed. For the moment it was more willing to go back where it'd come from.

46

The wolf's breath left me, and a bullet smacked into the bole of a tree near my head.

"Bitch! Bitch! You fucking bitch!"

I was shaking. The wolf's head hung heavy in my hands. My hands were wet and tacky with blood; it soaked my nightdress; it was in my mouth. There was an arm on the floor at my feet. Just an arm; nothing else. A nub of white bone showed through trailing red, wet laces of muscle, tendon, flesh. The knuckles were tattooed.

Small brass things glittered in the ground. They were bullet cases.

In my womb, the baby kicked.

"Bitch."

I heard a gun clicking; metallic sounds. I realised it was Blackthorn shouting. He was trying to reload.

"You bitch. You fucking bitch."

He was sobbing, and I was glad of it.

I wasn't in the clearing any more, but in the thick woods surrounding it. I crept through the trees, hissing through my teeth as sharp things cut my feet. But I wasn't unsteady, not any more.

A few yards from the clearing, I found Frank, or what was left of him. He had been opened up. His head was divorced from his body, lay nearby. He had no eyes. Or genitals. His gun hand, and gun, were gone.

I moved to the clearing's edge. Blackthorn stood in the middle of it, whirling this way and that. Dawn was starting to lighten the air; I crouched low, out of plain sight.

Near Blackthorn lay a one-armed torso; I couldn't see the rest of Tyler. Blackthorn's trousers steamed, and he was crying.

Weep, *Franquista*.

"Do you want to live, Blackthorn?" I called.

He spun, raising the gun.

"Don't fire another shot," I said. "Or you'll be like Tyler."

Blackthorn looked at the body and whimpered.

"If you want to live," I called, "do as I say."

"Alright." His voice was a sobbing croak.

"First," I said, "throw the gun away. Do it, now."

The pistol flickered into the undergrowth.

"Second," I said. "Do you remember the rules you told me before?"

"Yes."

"Repeat them."

"Answer … answer m-my questions. Don't lie. Don't try to trick me."

"Or?"

"Or-or-"

"Say it, Blackthorn."

"Or I'll hurt your husband."

"Good. The same rules apply to you, now, Blackthorn, except that if you break them … Blackthorn?"

"Yes?"

"Look at Tyler."

He did, and he whimpered again.

"Now – Blackthorn?"

"Yes."

"Is my husband still alive?"

"Yes. Yes."

"Take out your mobile phone, Blackthorn."

He did.

"Now you're going to call Max, and you're going to tell him to take our car and drive away. You're going to tell him not to harm Jim, to leave him alive. Do you understand?"

"Yes."

"Then do it."

He obeyed.

I watched him and I thought. Max was an irrelevance now, but Blackthorn? Too dangerous to leave alive. I'd have to find some story to tell the police, of course, but anything but the truth would suffice. I wasn't sure what I should, or could, tell Jim.

48

I wondered what the wolf's breath might have done to my unborn child; I could only hope his, or her, innocence would be of some protection.

How many times was too many times? Once? Twice? More, I was certain. Almost certain. I would rebury the wolf's head. Or hide it in a safer place. Perhaps closer to home, because the *Franquistas* are always with us, and they do not forget.

I would only use it once more. Only once.

I prayed I'd have the strength to keep my word to myself.

Blackthorn was whimpering again; I raised the wolf's lips to mine, and drew breath.

For Rebecca Ros.

PET

Gary Fry

"You won't even know I'm here, Mum," said Edgar, and hoped he told the truth. "I'll be in and out most days and I often work late at the office."

The last remark was inaccurate, of course, but he thought this was the only way he'd manage to survive staying with his mother two nights a week while working away from his seaside home.

"You'll have to bring Trudy and James one time," his mum replied in that smothering, deceptively grasping way she had – the way that had finally driven Edgar away from the city, several years ago. She'd transferred her affections to her husband, to Edgar's father, until he'd died a few months earlier, and now all she had was the familiar family dog. Edging out of the house, Edgar watched this beast in the garden. It cowered in its kennel, as if to say, *Don't leave me with her. I can't stand her neediness any more.* But Edgar had no choice. He'd only stopped by to drop off his overnight bag and was due at the office in half an hour.

"I'll see you tonight," he added, ignoring his mum's far from subtle prompt about him bringing his wife and son across from the coast one week. Trudy had difficulties with the older woman, too, and although James had rather enjoyed the excessive attention, that was surely only because Edgar hadn't allowed the boy too much exposure to it ... well, certainly nothing like the nightmarish ordeal he'd endured as a lad.

The front door creaked shut behind him – a devious sound representing his sneaky mother perfectly – and then Edgar strode past the poor, bony hound in its wooden home. "That's right, you poor little thing," he said, stooping briefly to pat the dog's hairy belly while covering his nose to deflect its rancid smell, "you stay where it's safe: away from *her.*"

And then he was away.

In all fairness, he reflected as he drove into the city centre, his circumstances could be a lot worse. After losing his job with the local council on the coast, he'd struggled to find work in the area and had had no choice but to take this one, seventy miles from his home yet situated in the place he'd grown up. Staying over a few nights a week with his mother was the only way he could make the post financially viable, what with the crippling price of petrol these days. And of course she was more than glad to have him.

His new job was relatively straightforward, just checking applications against a number of qualification criteria and entering any borderline cases into an automated computer system that generated a letter asking the client for more information. He could do this kind of thing with his eyes shut and often completed his tasks while maximising relaxation. This was a habit he'd developed over years in the same game. There was no point in getting stressed, particularly after all the weird dynamics involved in his childhood, some of which he would surely revisit during his stay here each week.

But he didn't want to think about that. Instead, towards the end of the day, he called his wife, who was fine and asked how he was coping so far. He knew very well she wasn't talking about his new job. They laughed quite a bit, as they always did, and then he hung up, hesitated a moment, and finally pecked in the digits of his mother's telephone number. The line rang for a while before being broken by a lengthy rasping sound that sounded almost … canine. However, after a brief ensuing silence, his mother said, "Hello?"

"Oh hi, Mum. Just thought I'd call and let you know that I'll be working late this evening. Still learning the ropes, you know. Thought I'd put in some extra hours, so I don't struggle to keep up later. A stitch in time and all that. See ya."

His mum only had to chance to say, "Okay, love. We'll wait up for you," before Edgar terminated the connection and got ready to go out for something to eat and drink.

By 'we', she'd meant the dog, of course. No doubt the poor

mutt had been let back inside after a night in the kennel to be pampered and snuggled and embraced all day long. Evolution had of course prepared dogs for this kind of attention, but surely even this affectionate species had its limits ... By now, Edgar was into his second pint, having already consumed a marvellous curry in a fine restaurant opposite the imposing monolith of his new workplace. Later, some lads, freshly changed from their office garments and reeking of sweet aftershave, came in and joined him for more drinks. They told humorous stories about the many stupid ways people had attempted to 'cheat the system'. Then, at about nine o'clock, Edgar decided to leave.

Yes, five pints was quite a lot to drive on, but he'd eaten a good meal before starting to drink and it was apparently true that the body processed a unit of alcohol every hour. He'd been out for four hours, so if one pint contained two units of alcohol and four had been processed, he'd already eliminated the effects of ... As he drove carefully along the dual carriageway towards his mother's place – his childhood home – he lost his grasp on this calculation and sensed old memories, ale-nurtured, come creeping back into his brain.

Back in the 1980s everything had started falling apart, at least according to Edgar's mother. Missing children, absent fathers, 'quickie' divorces, and many women preyed upon – all these things had terrified her, leading to a decidedly hands-on style of parenting. Edgar had been teased at school on account of the close attention his mum had shown, making him packed lunches and meeting him at the gates at the end of each day. He'd always had to be home before dark, too, which had played havoc with his social life. He didn't believe he'd ever fully recovered from this feeling of constant surveillance.

He parked the car in front of his mum's house, telling himself that the only face now looking at him, at nearly forty years of age, was that of the moon high above the property's roof, bathing the area in its stark glow. He swayed towards the front gate, automatically correcting his tipsy posture even though he'd made the journey without drawing the attention of police. Old habits died hard, however, and there were always other sources of discipline to placate.

His dad had never been much use, always spending his time out in his garden shed building the matchstick models he never showed to anyone other than Edgar. This had been their one common interest while living in a borderline autistic household in which one member controlled the social temperature, like a frugal bill payer with one hand on a central heating control and with a preference for a cool climate. Since marrying and having a child of his own, Edgar had sometimes wondered whether it was his dad's negligence that had led his mum to behave with such palpable neediness, but this sympathetic attitude had never lasted long. She was too frustratingly manipulative for that.

As he passed the dog's kennel – its tenant must be fast asleep, because despite his clumsily audible steps, there was no movement from within – Edgar drew breath before entering the house with the key his mother had given him that morning.

He found her in the lounge, waiting up just as she'd promised to. She'd obviously been doing something she felt embarrassed about, because as soon as he put his head around the door, she appeared to hide in her hands a few small objects she'd had positioned on the coffee table in front of her, on a dark tablecloth covered in quilted stars and ancient symbols.

More of her new age nonsense, Edgar thought, recalling his mother's interest in runes and the spirit world and even the afterlife. This was another reason people had shunned the family in the past. Edgar certainly didn't want to get into a conversation about all this stuff now.

He said, "Long day at the …" – he paused to belch – "… at the office. I'm exhausted. I'm going up to … to bed."

"Oh, I thought you might stay up a while and have a nice mug of malted milk with me, Eddie."

Mum, I'm not twelve, he wanted to yell back, releasing over twenty-five years of pent-up aggression, but he knew this wouldn't be worth it. She'd simply turn on the waterworks, the great punishing tears which, despite obviously being manufactured and manipulative, had never failed to evoke feelings of guilt in Edgar.

In the event, he said nothing, but this only prompted his mum to add more.

"It's been a while since we sat together and talked," she began, shuffling those hidden objects in her hands. "I thought we might discuss the old times."

But what was there to discuss? Nothing had ever happened back then, everything perceived as being too risky and warned against in no uncertain terms. Edgar didn't think he'd done anything adventurous until his late teens, after leaving home for a bedsit close to the college at which he'd studied. He certainly hadn't had a proper drink until this period, though he could admit to having made up for that since.

As the house around him gave another drunken lurch, he stepped back into the hallway, and although every fibre in his frame protested, a ruthlessly programmed part of him – the polite, obedient self his mother had conjured into being during years of exclusive access to his soul – replied, "Maybe tomorrow night, Mum. I need to get some sleep now."

And then he departed, stumbling upstairs to his childhood bedroom and to whatever subconscious material his mind seemed destined to dredge up for urgent analysis.

As it turned out, this was all quite commonplace stuff. He dreamed of a creature scuttling around the house, coming up the steps with hobbling uncertainty, prowling the upper level a little stiff-limbed, and nudging open one door after another, as if in search of either succour or sustenance. There was scent involved in this hapless audible fumbling – a funky animal smell, like old unwashed fur – and then visual aspects were added to the mix: the long, carpet-skirting bedroom curtains in Edgar's room stirred as this thing passed by, its nails or claws clicking against the sticks of furniture into which it blindly collided, before slinking once again through the doorway and into the hallway and then surely back downstairs.

It had just been the dog, of course – his mother's latest beloved pet. Upon waking the following morning, this was Edgar's fog-headed conclusion. He quickly searched the room and found a few strands of lengthy grey hair attached to the hem of his ruffled bed sheets. One of his dad's rules, to which his mum had been forced to adhere, involved no animals being allowed in the house overnight. That had been a point of principle for the ageing man, and although he'd been hectored and bullied in almost all other matters, this single stipulation – the one that perhaps distinguished him as a master in his own home – had remained ironclad.

Since his death, however, Edgar's mother had clearly overruled this, and the furtive beast hunting the house last night must have been the poor animal that now suffered the terrors of its owner's cloying focus.

As Edgar dressed for another day in the office, he recalled often seeking recourse to the dog owned by the family when he was a child. This had been a short-haired mongrel, and not the mangy mutt his mother currently owned. Whenever tensions had run high in the house – each subtle enough not to be perceived by outsiders – Edgar had clung to the dog, holding its comfortingly warm body until his mum had sent it outside at bedtime, shifting both Edgar's and her matchstick model-building husband's focus onto her. There'd been no escape.

When Edgar stepped across the landing, he heard his mother muttering something drowsily from beyond the closed door of her own room. She must be still asleep and dreaming of when Edgar's dad had been alive, because her comments took the form of, "I've missed your cuddles," and "It's good to have you back in my arms." Or maybe she was just talking to the dog, which had presumably settled on her bed after all its restless antics overnight.

Whatever the truth was, Edgar was grateful to stray downstairs and make a swift beeline for the front entrance. Before reaching it, however, he caught sight of something in the lounge – an old looking book with what appeared to be Latin text on the front. *E MORTUIS REVOCO*, the title read, and the whole tome looked like some kind of guide to achieving something forbidden and abstruse … Alongside the book were a number of herbs and powders, which made Edgar think of his wife's penchant for cooking and all the fine meals she prepared him. *Just one more night to survive here*, he reflected, looking forward to returning to the coast for the weekend. He thought he and the family could take a trip somewhere fun, somewhere lacking all the lugubrious atmosphere of his mum's creepy residence.

He stepped outside, and soon heard the dog shuffling its old bones out of its rickety kennel. The scrawny thing looked as if it had slept extremely deeply and without disturbance … but how could that be so when Edgar had clearly heard it scampering sluggishly around the house? He must have been dreaming, he decided, just as his mother surely was now upstairs. He turned to look at her bedroom window and saw a face looking out at him, which only after a few seconds' sustained attention did he realise was actually just a patch of condensation rested on the glass like a mass of whitish hair.

Feeling uncomfortable for no tangible reason, Edgar left the garden, picked a few grey hairs from his hands that had stuck to them when he had stroked the dog, and finally got inside his car.

After starting the engine and flicking on the wipers he noticed that some bastard had bent one of the blades, making it scratch his windscreen with an irritating grinding sound. Young vandals, he decided, taking a sharp right into the high street that would deliver him directly to the city centre. At least his childhood had furnished him with a few manners and a little respect. He couldn't be completely dismissive of the way his mother had brought him up. He'd tried to pass on similar standards to his own lad, though had consciously extracted all the weird family dynamics from which he'd suffered as a child. That was normal parenting, wasn't it? Maintaining what was good about the way you'd been brought up while eradicating the bad points. If this attempt at incremental enhancement was true, however, why did everything appear to be getting worse in the world? Edgar glanced again at his broken windscreen wiper snatching off freckles of rain. This culture, he reflected with some dismay; it lacks discipline.

He spent the rest of the day assisting the welfare state to compensate for what so many individuals were unable to handle, and when it was time to leave he felt more apprehensive than reluctant about returning so early to his childhood home. His mother would be waiting, of course, and had perhaps even made him another of her unappealing meals. It would be just like the old days, except of course for the absence of Dad ... But all these thoughts served only to make Edgar feel even more uncomfortable about visiting the house, let alone sleeping there overnight.

In the event, he decided to call and explain that he had to work overtime again and that he'd grab something to eat from the office vending machine. She answered on the third ring ... or at least someone did. When Edgar said, "Hello? *Hello?*" with increasing impatience and unease, it was several seconds before his mum finally came on the line with the words, "Thank you, dear."

What was she thanking him for? And why had Edgar just heard footsteps approaching the phone from inside the house? For some surreally disquieting reason, Edgar's mind had conjured up an image of his mother's ageing dog, standing up on its weak back legs and holding out the phone for her with its two front paws ... But that had been stupid, *stupid.*

He told his mum what he planned, and when she expressed predictable concerns about a lack of nutrients in the kind of food he might acquire from an office machine, he promised to get an apple, too, and a diet drink. Then he hung up, shaken and bemused.

The world had developed a solution for such dilemmas, of course, and its name was ale. Over an Italian meal Edgar downed four pints, sent his wife an alcohol-sweetened text, tried to marshal so many nebulous fears deep in his mind, and finally drove back to the home he really mustn't start thinking of again as his *home*.

After parking up in the street, he was accosted by one of the neighbours as soon as he got out of the car. He knew this excitable old lady from previous social gatherings, when his parents had had a few friends round for drinks. Edgar had hated these occasions, as had his wife Trudy, though their son James had seemed happy enough, having been treated and pampered by the likes of the woman now sizing up to Edgar as if he was some kind of petty burglar. But then she appeared to recognise him.

"Oh, it's *you*," she said, her seventy- or eighty-year-old face flexing with innumerable wrinkles. Her rheumy eyes, flashing dully in moonlight, didn't seem very strong, and her tiny body dressed in a plastic jacket hardly seemed equipped to deal with the kind of hoodlum who'd damaged Edgar's car overnight. Nevertheless, she said, "We've had a bit of trouble around here lately. We're mostly old ladies in these houses now. So it's nice to have a young man around for a while."

"Well, I'm only staying here a few days a week," Edgar was eager to inform the woman, who looked a tad senile, her expression misting over with confusion.

"Yes, I saw you earlier today," she went rabidly on, and then turned to point at his mother's house – at the window of the master bedroom currently filled with heavy curtains. "In daylight, this would be. Just after breakfast. But ... the old glass made your face appear *different*." She was now rising to her surely deluded theme, her hands fidgeting furtively. "It looked all cracked up like ... well, like your *father's* used to be. And that big white beard he ... I mean *you* were wearing was obviously just ... just ..."

"Condensation on the glass," Edgar was happy to inform her, and was then relieved to enter the garden and hurry up the path. On this occasion there was no sign of the dog in its kennel; perhaps his mother had already let the beast in for the night.

The neighbour had simply got her times mixed up, that was all. Maybe she'd seen Edgar standing at his old bedroom window next to the master's one, when he'd spent a few minutes that morning searching the room for evidence of any nocturnal activity. He remembered parting the curtains to check the low-set window for signs of a wet nose having been pressed against it. There'd been nothing, of course, but this would certainly account for the old woman's misperception.

And now Edgar had another ageing lady to deal with. As he crept beyond the lounge doorway, he saw his mother seated on the couch, this time without any of the weird accoutrements she'd been handling the previous evening. She looked forlorn and terribly lonely, and just for a moment Edgar felt a little guilty at the way he'd always treated her. She'd lived by herself for over five months now, ever since his father had died – the husband she'd clung desperately to, until fate had at last got one up on her.

As Edgar was about to speak, he heard a sound from elsewhere. At first he'd assumed this furtive thump had come from inside the property – from the cellar perhaps, whose door behind him in the hallway was shut, with a key hanging out of its lock – though closer analysis suggested it might have come from outside. Had it been the youths the uppity neighbour had bemoaned, come to cause more damage? Edgar hoped not, and realised that this was more than concern about his car. Although there was no way he'd ever consider spending more time here than he had to, he didn't wish his mother any harm. He hoped she'd be all right.

He said, "Are you … are you okay, Mum?"

She glanced up, a little startled, as if she hadn't heard him arrive or had perhaps been expecting someone else to come creeping through the doorway – a *person* to judge by her elevated gaze, which was angled way above a dog's height. She looked disturbed, as if whatever hope she'd been harbouring since he'd arranged to come and stay was waxing and waning like the mysterious activities of the moon.

"All I ever wanted was a normal family life," she said, her voice gravelly and ghosted – the sound of age and all its attendant despair. "I just wanted us all to be happy together."

If she was talking about Edgar and his father, Edgar found this claim outlandish. The old man had never been intimate with either him or his mother, and the only childhood affection Edgar had ever received was from the family dog. He'd sought human alternatives as an adult – a wife and a son with whom he'd avoided making the same mistakes his mother had while living with two others, each tuned out from life by the insidious influence of such a needy wife and mother. It had all been almost vampirical.

Feeling bitter again, he left her and retreated upstairs. A little later, after listening for intruders outside and hearing nothing other than a vague scratching noise he ascribed to the dog shuffling in its kennel, he fell asleep and dreamed of three people stitched together like thick material, flesh bound to flesh bound to flesh by great sewn loops of sharp wire ... Then these dark imaginings moved on, to register a fresh violation from something light, squat and wily. This thing shifted to and fro in the room he occupied, unseen on the floor. A moment later, however, Edgar sensed it latch onto the sheets he was now using to defend himself against the attention of whatever approached, bearing such an earthy, bestial scent ... Here it came, still invisible because he had his eyes closed, clawing up the side of the bed and up onto the mattress, to settle lengthily, like some rotting log, alongside one of his legs. He reached out a hand, felt for the beast. It was dry, like old fur. And the softness of this excessive facial hair – it was just the dog, of course – eventually nursed him back to sleep.

Next he dreamed of his father, come back from the dead to visit him ... After that nightmare, Edgar snapped open his eyes. Immediately he heard noises from elsewhere in the property. He listened carefully, still sensing that firm presence along the length of one leg. Were these sounds coming from downstairs ... or outside? Surely if the dog was on the bed with him, anyone in the garden would be an unwelcome visitor. Indeed, he wasn't the only one to have detected this intrusion: the dog started barking. The fact that it hadn't moved from its prostrate position on the bed didn't trouble Edgar, especially when he realised that the sounds of its protest were muffled, as if shielded by something considerably solid – a wall. He was yet to wake up properly; that was why all his senses were affected in this way.

He sat up, shaking meddlesome fragments of his dreams from his mind. But now here came something to remind him inexorably of all those fearful imaginings: footsteps from outside his room. His father, was this, come to haunt him from beyond the grave? But what a foolish thought that was! Nevertheless, as the unsteady pacing grew nearer and nearer the closed doorway – was this person coming upstairs or rather crossing the hallway out there? – this disturbing interpretation became difficult to resist.

Edgar found himself instinctively reaching out, just as he had as a child, for the dog on the bed pressed against one leg. Once he'd blindly taken hold of it, he felt its bony body and mangy fur, yet he continued to pull it his way, bringing it closer to his face. It was still barking, though that didn't make any sense at all, because although these canine exclamations were now bright and crisp in the late night, they didn't appear to be coming from anywhere near Edgar. In fact, they were coming from outside the house, from the garden where the kennel was. Perhaps vandals had now returned and his mother's dog was doing its worst to see them off ...

But who would now see off Edgar's intruder.

The bedroom door several yards in front of him began to open.

Edgar held on tighter to whatever scabrous travesty he was clutching in his adult arms.

And when his mother finally appeared in the opening and

said, "Back together at last. Just one happy family," it took Edgar several seconds to slacken his hold and look at the slack-limbed, hirsute, stinking person from whom he'd never sought such reassuring comfort in the past.

ASHES TO ASHES

David Williamson

Thump, thump, thump! Ann Clarke banged on the bathroom door with her fist. Her husband had been in there, running water almost nonstop for over forty minutes.

"How much bloody *longer* are you gonna be in there? I have to get to work too, you know!"

Moments later, Steve Clarke slid back the bolt on the bathroom door and emerged from the steam-filled room clad in his dressing gown, his head swathed in a large white towel.

"'Bout bleedin' time too!" Mrs Clarke brushed roughly past him, and slammed the door behind her.

When she returned to their bedroom, some fifteen minutes later, Steve was sitting on their double bed, still wearing his gown, with the towel draped over his head like a prizefighter.

"You're gonna be late!" snapped Ann, doing up her bra before stepping into her underwear. In fact, she was completely dressed and starting her morning make up ritual, before she realised that her husband hadn't replied or stirred from his position on the edge of the bed.

She finally relented. "You alright?"

Steve Clarke replied by way of removing the white towel covering his head, and as he did so, a shower of white flaky material fluttered from the towel and wafted gently, before settling on the duvet.

Ann let out a low whistle. "Bloody hell, Steve! That's some dandruff you have there." She took a couple of steps closer to examine him further.

His still damp hair contained a mass of large white flakes, and there was what could best be described as a 'tide mark' of red, angry looking skin, which appeared to cover his entire scalp and end in an almost straight line just above his eyebrows.

"I just woke up like this, Annie. The more I wash it, the

worse it gets," he said, at last. There was a look of near panic in his eyes as his wife studied her husband's flaking, raw looking scalp.

"Blimey! I dunno *what* it could be, Steve. Some kind of psoriasis maybe?" she offered and then shrugged.

"Psoriasis?" he almost whined. "Is that *serious*?" he added, eyes wide as he pulled the towel over his head once more.

Ann touched his shoulder before noticing that it had a fine layer of dead skin cells dusting it, and quickly removed her hand again without thinking.

"Well … it's probably more serious than man flu. Longer lasting at least."

Steve let out a startled whimper like a small child before she continued. "But I'm sure they have creams and stuff these days that'll soon clear it up. Take the morning off and go see the doctor, would be my advice."

Two hours later Steve was sitting in the doctor's waiting room, his head covered by his old Beanie hat pulled tightly over his crusty scalp and a pair of large, aviator style sunglasses hiding his eyes, the collar of his jacket flapped up around his neck. He couldn't help noticing that the other patients were casting him sideways looks. Although the waiting room was crowded, the seats to either side of him were vacant as though people would rather stand and wait than sit near him.

After what seemed like hours, his name was called and he stood up in a shower of flaky skin. There was an almost audible sigh throughout the waiting room as he left.

"Sit down … Mr … er … Clarke. Now … what seems to be the problem?" the doctor asked, pen poised and ready over his prescription pad.

Steve sat down nervously and removed his hat and sunglasses to yet another small blizzard of dead skin particles.

The doctor looked up from his prescription pad for the first time and his patient could see the undisguised look of horror on the medical man's face.

"Oh!" he said, simply, making no attempt to move from his position behind his desk. "And how long have you been like this, may I ask?"

Where the 'tide mark' of red had stopped at his eyebrows only two hours earlier, it now continued down to just below his top lip and what had been sore and angry-looking skin before, had now become white, flaky and almost scaly in appearance.

"Well, Doctor, I woke up this morning with an itchy head, and now it's like this." and as if to emphasise the problem, another storm of white skin cells wafted from his head as he spoke.

"I see," replied the doctor, but it was patently clear from the expression on his face, that he really had no idea what he was dealing with.

His hand moved spider-like across the prescription pad and he continued speaking as he wrote, without looking up at his patient again.

"We'll try you on this. Actually it's a mixture of several things used in the treatment of psoriasis, eczema and other skin conditions, and we'll see how you go on that. If things don't improve within a week, I'll have to get you looked at by a skin specialist at the allergy clinic; okay, Mr ... er ... Clarke?" and with that, he tore the prescription from his pad and handed it to his patient, before busying himself with some apparently very urgent paperwork.

Steve Clarke pulled his hat over his scaly scalp, popped on his sunglasses and silently left the surgery. But not before hearing on his way out:

"Nurse, could you pop in here with the Hoover, please?" over the intercom.

By the time he'd had his prescription filled, at no small expense, and had returned home, the 'rash' or whatever it was, had now crept down to the base of his neck and was starting to reach down towards his chest.

When Ann got in from work, she found her husband lying in

their bed and covered in some sort of greasy, oily substance. Large areas of his hair appeared to have fallen out in clumps, and what remained was plastered to his totally white and scaly scalp.

Amazingly, even though he was coated in the unctuous ointment, his skin was somehow still managing to shed flakes, and the floor on his side of the bed was several millimetres deep in dead cells, the duvet and his pillow were a complete mess.

"Oh my God, Steve! What the hell did the doctor say?" she was trying to exude calm, but the nightmare vision of her husband lying in the bed shedding hair and skin, did little to help her bedside manner.

Steve had been dozing, and awoke with a start.

"Oh, hi, darling. You okay?" he slurred, drowsily.

Ann wanted to sit on the bed beside him, she wanted to stroke his face and comfort him, but she couldn't bring herself to do either.

"Never mind about *my* day, what did the doctor say? You look awful!" she blurted, immediately regretting saying those last words.

Steve tried to sit upright, but after struggling for a few seconds he sighed and gave up.

"He didn't really seem to know, but thought it was probably something like psoriasis as you said, and he prescribed me all these ointments." He waved a scaly hand towards the various bottles and tubes of medication littering his bedside table, adding, "It seems to have got a bit worse since then, so I phoned the surgery about an hour ago to make another appointment, but apparently the doctor's gone sick now, and no one can see me until next week."

Ann looked appalled, and she stormed across to the phone on her side of the bed.

"I'm calling for an ambulance; this is bloody ridiculous!"

Steve made another massive effort to raise himself from the bed.

"No! I don't want an ambulance," he wailed, "just give this cream time to start working, and I'll be fine," he added, pleadingly, and against her better judgement, his wife stopped with her hand hovering above the receiver.

"If you're not starting to improve by the morning, it's the hospital for you; and no arguing!"

Steve tried to smile, but his lips were too cracked and scaly.

"Fair enough, Annie, but let's just see what happens, okay?"

As much as she would have liked to have snuggled up to her husband that night, Ann simply couldn't bring herself to share a bed with him, let alone touch him, and therefore she slept in the spare room.

She had looked in on him before going to bed herself, but he'd been fast asleep and she'd thought it better to let him rest.

He was still flat out when she bustled in with a mug of coffee the next morning and asked softly, "Morning, darling. How are you feeling today?"

No reply.

Ann went over and opened the heavy curtains, flooding the bedroom with morning sunlight. But Steve still hadn't stirred in the bed.

She could just see the top of his head poking out as she crossed to the bed. She reached out and drew back the duvet to be greeted by a completely fleshless, grinning skull that lay amongst several inches of dry, dead skin cells.

Without thinking, she continued to pull back the bed covers, and as the scream formed in her throat, she realised that her husband's entire body was now nothing more than skeletal bones lying amongst a hideous dust composed of dried skin, and human organs.

As the terrified scream finally broke from her throat, she realised with dawning horror, that her own head had now started itching badly.

THE APPRENTICE

Anna Taborska

Ralph baked bread. It was a strange feeling – using those massive, clumsy knuckles to knead the soft dough rather than to rain down the wrath of God on the head of anyone who gave him a funny look. A strange feeling to have people smile at him trustingly and talk to him about the weather while they waited for him to wrap the warm scented bread, rather than cross the road when they saw him coming. Yes, it was a piece of good fortune that Ralph had picked up a little of the trade from his mother before his father had battered her to death. And lucky too that Ralph had chanced upon the village just at the time when their baker had gone for a walk and been found beaten to a pulp on the side of the road. Not that Ralph claimed to know anything about that.

Ralph's customers were very fond of his braided loaves and animal shapes, but Ralph's real speciality – and his own particular favourite – were the little heart-shaped buns. Ralph's heart-shaped buns were the talk of the village, and people came from miles around to buy them for their sweethearts, their spouses or their children.

Ralph didn't have any children, a sweetheart or a spouse, nor did he feel any need for them. As far as he could tell, children were always wailing or causing mischief, and women were always nagging or demanding money from their long-suffering husbands. No, what Ralph really wanted was an apprentice – someone who would help around the bakery; someone to whom Ralph could impart his knowledge, whom he could nurture, and kick the shit out of now and again when he got annoyed and needed to let off a little steam. That was what Ralph wanted. It would be kind of like playing God.

Then one day Ralph's prayers were answered. It was hard to tell the boy's age; he was slight and pale, with a mop of unruly dark hair. He could have been twenty or he could have been twelve; there was no way to find out as the boy never spoke a word. He turned up one evening, just as it was getting dark, with a sign around his neck that read, 'I will work for food and lodgings'. Not only was the boy mute, but Ralph's attempts to communicate with him by way of a quill and some parchment led the baker to believe that he couldn't read or write either. Luckily for Ralph, the boy didn't appear to be deaf, and responded to Ralph's invitation to sit down and eat by doing just that.

There was a hint of desperation in the speed with which the boy wolfed down his food, and something pitiful in the way he threw Ralph an occasional sideways glance, as if worried that the man would take the food away before he had devoured it all. Ralph felt a confusing mixture of pity and annoyance – a feeling that would grow over the coming weeks – and barely resisted the urge to tear the bowl away from the boy before he had finished eating.

After supper, Ralph took the boy to the small barn that used to house his horse – before he'd flogged it to death – and told the boy that he could sleep there and start work the following morning. The boy looked at Ralph and nodded. And so it was that Ralph got himself an apprentice.

That night Ralph had trouble falling asleep and, when he finally did, he dreamt that he was on a scaffold, about to be executed. He was protesting his innocence, but nobody seemed to care; they just shoved a gag in his mouth and hanged him anyway. Ralph woke up the next morning with a stiff neck and a splitting headache. He could still feel that terrible burning sensation of the hangman's rope biting, and he was in a foul mood. Then he remembered the boy. He strode to the barn and saw him fast asleep in the hay.

"Get up, you lazy shit!" Ralph kicked the bale of hay that the boy was lying on. The boy fell off, eyes wide with surprise, then got up and walked out of the barn, towards Ralph's house, which doubled up as the village bakery. Something about the calmness in the boy's stride annoyed the hell out of Ralph.

"Watch and learn," hissed Ralph, and proceeded to mix and knead the dough for the day's bread before shaping it and placing it carefully in the large oven. When he was done with the morning's baking, Ralph ordered the boy to clean up the bakery before the first customers arrived.

"Who's this?" Ralph's customers gazed curiously at the shy young man cowering in the corner.

"That's my new apprentice." Ralph beamed.

"Where'd he come from?"

"Oh … He's my cousin's boy."

"Never knew you had a cousin, Ralph."

"Aye, I do … She asked me to train him to be a baker."

"I see … He doesn't say much, does he?"

"No, he doesn't at that." And that's when Ralph realised the beauty of his situation. The boy would never talk back, never contradict him, never complain.

After the last of the customers had left, and Ralph had closed up for the day, he put out two plates of food. The boy approached the table cautiously. Ralph let him sit down and reach a hand out towards the plate. "No!" he shouted, and pulled the plate away roughly. "You clean up and then you eat!"

Ralph watched the boy wipe down the work surfaces and sweep up the spilt flour. The boy was so pale and skinny. There was something unsavoury about him – unhealthy – rather like a mangy dog. When the boy got close to Ralph while sweeping, his back to the baker, Ralph surprised both of them by kicking him. The boy sprawled on the floor, then picked himself up silently and continued sweeping. Ralph laughed. "You can eat now," he told the boy, and left the room.

The next day Ralph got up earlier than usual and was on his

way to kick the boy awake, but found him already waiting on the doorstep.

"Oh, you're up." Ralph let the boy in. "In that case, you can show me what you learned yesterday about making bread." Ralph watched as the boy mixed the flour and water, and kneaded the dough carefully.

"Not like that, you have to do it harder." Ralph put his large hand over the boy's wrist, intending to help him knead the dough, but somehow the feel of that thin, cold small hand brought about the irresistible urge to crush, pulverise, destroy. He suddenly needed to hear bones cracking and feel the little digits turn to jelly in his grasp. The boy winced in pain, but didn't cry out. Ralph stopped abruptly and let go of the boy's hand, wondering just how much damage he'd done, afraid that the boy might not be able to work. The boy held his limp hand, but soon moved his fingers a little, assuring Ralph that he'd stopped in time and there was no real injury.

"That's enough now. Go and sweep the floor." The boy did as he was told, largely using his other hand to hold the broom.

Ralph couldn't really complain about the boy's work. He kept the bakery clean, he did a good enough job with the dough and the animal shapes and even the hearts, but there was something in his manner that Ralph found irritating. Maybe it was the lack of enthusiasm. There was something amazing about making bread to feed people, but from the absence of emotion in the boy's face, Ralph was sure that he didn't feel that wonder at all. Somewhere at the back of Ralph's mind floated the notion that perhaps he could beat the wonder into the boy.

As the days passed, Ralph's customers noticed that his new apprentice seemed to have a knack for acquiring black eyes and fresh bruises on a regular basis.

"He's very clumsy," Ralph explained. "If there's a door, you can guarantee he'll walk right into it. If there's something lying on the ground, you can rest assured he'll trip over it and fall flat on his face." Ralph's customers sympathised with the baker – it must be hard for the man having such a clumsy apprentice, and it wasn't like he could sack him, the boy being his cousin's child and all.

After three weeks of beatings, the boy's face remained emotionless. He took punishment with the same apparent stoicism as he took the extremely rare praise bestowed on him by the baker. Occasionally the boy would look at Ralph with a dispassion that drove the man to increasing acts of violence.

One evening when the boy was waiting for the bread stove to cool down so that he could clean it, Ralph grabbed him and shoved his head in the oven. The heat was insufficient to do any serious harm, but it must have hurt. The boy resisted only for the briefest moment – an instinctive reaction born of surprise, but then went totally limp in the baker's powerful arms, and Ralph was able to push him headfirst into the hot dark space.

"Scream, you fuck, scream!" shouted Ralph. But the boy didn't scream and didn't struggle. When Ralph finally pulled him out again, the boy's face was bright red, and sweat and tears were streaming down it. The boy swooned a little, but remained standing, gazing at Ralph with what at first glance appeared to be the same blank expression he normally wore. Then for a moment, in the flicker of the candlelight, Ralph thought that the corners of the boy's mouth had turned up just a little, but no – surely it was just a trick of the light and shadows playing around the room.

"You want to act like a dumb animal, you'll be treated like a dumb animal." Ralph marched the boy to the barn and fetched an old dog chain lying in the corner. He brandished it at the boy, but the boy didn't flinch. Unnerved, Ralph chained the boy and tethered him in the barn. You never knew what was going on in that scrawny head of his. Perhaps behind that stoic facade he was hatching some elaborate escape plan. It was best to err on the side of prudence.

From that time on, Ralph would chain the boy up at night,

releasing him to carry out his chores during the day. He cut down on his meals too, as depriving him of food seemed to be the only thing that elicited any reaction from the boy, in the form of the slightest hint of a frown.

One day Ralph entered the barn and noticed a foetid smell, as if a rodent had died somewhere in the hay and was starting to rot. He looked around, and finally realised that the putrid stench was emanating from the boy. The metal chain had been cutting into the boy's ankle and the flesh had started to fester. Ralph understood the danger of infection, and took the boy into the house, to disinfect the wound.

As the baker swabbed the wound with alcohol, he looked at the boy's emaciated body, the bruises all over his arms and legs, and felt an unfamiliar twang of guilt. He looked up from the boy's infected ankle and saw the boy gazing at him with those dispassionate brown eyes. As had happened so many times before, rage at the boy's passivity and acceptance of his situation quickly replaced any pity the baker might have felt.

"What are you staring at?" The boy lowered his gaze, but it was too late; Ralph could feel the unstoppable fury growing inside him and he grabbed his horsewhip. By the time the red mist had cleared, Ralph realised he was still seeing red, as the boy was lying on the floor in a pool of his own blood.

"Oh my God, oh my God!" For the first time since he was twelve – and had broken his father's favourite pipe – Ralph started to panic. He remembered his dream and the stinging feeling of the noose around his neck. He threw the whip into a corner and knelt beside the unconscious boy. "I'm sorry. I'm so sorry! Oh please God don't let him be dead. Oh please don't be dead. I'll never lay a finger on you again, I swear!" Ralph knelt beside the boy and wept.

After what seemed like a very long time, the boy coughed, fresh blood spattering from his mouth and joining with the blood already on the floor. "Thank God, thank God." Ralph wanted to carry the boy to his bed, and reached out to touch him, but thought better of it. "Stay here. Don't move. I'm going to fetch the doctor."

When Ralph got back with the doctor, the boy was quite still once more.

"Good God!" The doctor hurried over to the boy. "What happened?"

"I don't know." Ralph squirmed as the doctor eyed him suspiciously. "He's free to do what he wants on Sunday. He went off to the neighbouring village, I think, and next thing I know he staggers in and collapses. I think he was attacked." The doctor gazed at Ralph for a moment longer, then turned back to the boy, carefully examining his head, back and chest.

"He's taken a severe beating. He has broken ribs and a broken arm. If his wounds get infected, he will die." The devastated expression on Ralph's face dispelled any suspicions the doctor might have had about the baker's guilt in the boy's predicament. "He can't be transported anywhere. I'll try to make him as comfortable as I can here, and you send for his mother."

"I'll take care of him." The doctor looked at Ralph in surprise. "I mean, his little brother and sister are very sick. My cousin can't leave them. Look, just tell me what to do and I'll look after him."

Ralph nursed the boy for many weeks. He cut down his opening hours and reduced the number of orders he took in. He would get through the baking and the selling as fast as he could, then spend the rest of the day and much of the night sitting by the boy, listening to his laboured breathing and hoping that his heart wouldn't stop. But it wasn't just fear of death – should he be found guilty of the boy's murder – that so unsettled Ralph. He had taken life before, but now for the first time he felt remorse.

The boy drifted in and out of consciousness. The doctor came by regularly to check on him and bring more medicine. Customers were complaining that Ralph's little heart-shaped buns didn't taste as good as they used to – it was as if the heart had gone out of making them.

Then one day, having apologised to the comatose boy a hundred times and cried himself to sleep the night before, Ralph awoke to find the boy sitting up in bed, watching him. Startled, Ralph started mumbling incoherent apologies, "Forgive me, please forgive me."

The boy dropped his gaze from Ralph's face and reached slowly and painfully for the edge of the bedclothes, pulling them off himself. Then equally slowly and painfully, he swung his legs out of bed and tentatively put his weight on them.

Ralph looked on in amazement and trepidation as the boy got out of bed and walked stiffly across the room, to the far corner. Leaning on the wall for support, the boy bent down cautiously and retrieved something from the floor. As Ralph watched, too shocked to move, the boy came towards him, one painful step at a time. When he was right in front of the trembling baker, the boy lifted his functioning arm, holding out the object he had picked up from the floor. Ralph looked down to see the horsewhip; the boy was holding it by the whipping end, offering the handle to Ralph to grasp. As Ralph looked in horror from the whip to the boy, for the first time since he had come into Ralph's home the apprentice's face broke out in a smile.

LIFE EXPECTANCY

Sam Dawson

Only other people find interesting things in attics.

Really. They do. Gas masks and tin helmets, horned gramophones, oil lamps, dusty paintings that are unexpectedly worth a fortune, service revolvers so old you're actually allowed to keep them.

Even boxes of toys or Wade Whimsies, which is what Judy spent her childhood hoping to discover every time her family moved and she investigated a new attic or basement or tumbledown shed. Exploring with a child's eyes of wonder that turned a stored piano stool's clawed feet peeking out from under a dustsheet into the beckoning appendages of a mythical beast. In her early teens it was Arthur Rackham illustrated books she hoped for, in her mid-teens a Miss Havisham Victorian wedding dress that, by the end of her teens, she would probably have dyed black.

People do find those kinds of things. Pick up a paper. Watch *Antiques Roadshow*. You'll see. It happens. To other people.

Other people, not Judy. Not so far, anyway. She blamed bad luck for it. Or maybe insulation and rewiring and woodworm and house clearances, all of which involve someone else thrusting inspection lamps into the darkest corners of loft and attic and under-eaves and discovering minor wonders, the kind of old and interesting things she loved but couldn't afford.

It wasn't greed on her part. Just that feeling that something is more magical if you discover it and clean it up yourself rather than buying it.

Which meant she had no great expectations of the attic above her and Cress and Toni's little rented part of the once splendid Victorian building overlooking the park into which they had just moved.

She had to look, though, even before they had quite finished stacking their boxes of Blu-rays and microwave curries and packets of spaghetti and bin bags of clothes and CDs and iPods and PS3 games and even a few of the textbooks that they were supposed to be studying.

They had half of the top floor, the tiny rooms that once would have accommodated the house's servants, made tinier by successive conversions into more and more compact flats and bedsits. Theirs was the first to be completed, still smelt strongly of paint, and was denuded of everything that might give it character by its all-over coat of magnolia, uniform Ikea and Lidl fittings, and its thin partition walls, which separated three boxy bedrooms, a shower room and a tiny kitchen with breakfast bar and built-in microwave.

The rest of the house was still unlet and undergoing its latest subdivision. Access to their flat was via a narrow, almost hidden-as-if-through-shame, servants' staircase. Below it was different. The ground and first floors were where the owners would have lived, and even though they were dotted with paint tins, ladders and roller trays, you could see how very grand they must once have been. For them the staircase was wide and proud, with solid balustrades and filials. The doors were high and broad and carved, and would have opened onto drawing and dining and billiard rooms, each of which now housed a soon-to-be completed flatlet.

There were no high ceilings and great sash windows up here though. Judy could reach the loft hatch just by standing on one of the kitchen stools. She pushed it open and swung herself up and in.

There was a light. It showed a narrow, low void. The insulation looked new, and bright little cutoffs of copper wire and bits of flex scattered on it showed that it was newly rewired. There was little chance of finding anything. Judy somehow just knew that the others were probably expecting her to be making the first coffees in their new flat, so it was important that they thought she was seeing if there was storage room for their empty suitcases and surplus George Foreman grills, rather than treasure hunting. She quickly, if painfully, crawled across the joists on her knees.

As she expected, nothing. Beyond the usual thrown away ends of copper pipe and an empty wasps' nest.

Along one wall several old pipes ran, all tightly bound in ancient sacking to stop them freezing. Probably defunct, but no one had wanted to take the risk of sawing through them and finding that one still held water.

Hardly worth checking. But she did.

Oh, wow. Right there where it must have become wedged between them and the wall when the attic had been cleared of junk. A wooden box. Judy tried to free it from above but it was trapped. Tugging at it made the old lead pipes bend and flex and she was frightened one would split and flood the place. She knelt back, thought about it a bit more and then tried again, this time pushing one hand into the itchy glass fibre insulation and under the pipe, while using the other from above to ease it free a centimetre at a time.

"Judy? We've nearly finished down here. We're about ready for a coffee." It was Toni's voice and Judy didn't need to be studying literature like Toni was to identify the subtext in that statement. If you want it make it yourself, she thought, I'm not your bloody servant. But what she called down was "Just a minute", while she tried to speed up the extrication of the box.

Then she had it free. Or nearly free, a cord trailed from it to behind the pipe. When she tugged on it, it came loose, revealing a metal and Bakelite earpiece at the other end. She turned the box over. It was a telephone. A wood and brass one, with a little arm out the side from which the earpiece hung, and a little metal horn into which you'd speak. A phone. An Edwardian or Victorian phone. How cool was that? If the roof had been high enough to allow it she'd probably have skipped downstairs with joy. Dusty though she was she made the coffee contendedly, barely able to take her gaze away from her find and happily unfazed by her flatmates' complete indifference to it.

It was about twelve centimetres high and more or less the

same wide, and a pleasing, heavily varnished walnut colour. Dusty and age-tarnished, but cleanable. She decided there'd be time to have a proper look later after the celebratory moving in takeaway that Cress had just phoned for. Then her mobile rang.

"Judy. Shao Li called in sick. We're shorthanded. We need you in tonight." It was Anne, the manager of the restaurant where she worked evenings as a waitress, washer up and general dogsbody. Where her pay came mainly in tips, which is to say, in a cheap pizza parlour aimed mainly at students, very little of it came in at all.

"Um, I'm just about to have dinner, Anne. I've just moved into a new flat today ... and ... couldn't Sean do it?"

Mistake. Sean worked half the hours and half as hard as anyone for the same pay. He was Anne's favourite, and dangled the possibility of an affair that would never happen in front of her, making her blind to the faults that were all too evident to the rest of the workforce. She responded angrily: "Look, Judy, you'd better decide and decide now. Do you want this job? Or not?"

Judy looked down the stairs and out through the flat's front door, left open so they'd hear the takeaway delivery driver. Night had fallen and not only did she not fancy going out onto the ill-lit streets bordering the park but she didn't even much fancy descending into the black, unheated emptiness of the main body of the house. Beyond their little hall everything was unlit and looming and she still hadn't learned the position of the widely spaced switches that gave you thirty seconds of light in which to find the next one.

"Well?" her boss demanded. She remembered a saying of her father's: 'Why don't you shove a broom up my arse and I'll sweep the floor while I'm at it', but what she actually replied was a timid: "Yes, Anne, I'll leave now."

The money for the conversion ran out, or the painters did. The rest of the house remained empty, at least for now. The girls finished moving in, put up posters, appropriated cabinets for their kitchen goods, labelled their food, and set the limits of how much time they'd stand the others occupying the bathroom. It was days before Judy had a moment to examine her find properly.

She found that it was hinged on one side and secured shut with a screw, which yielded to a bit of 3-In-One and the screwdriver her father had given her. He might be an old-fashioned sod when it came to expecting his wife to do all the 'women's work' around the home, but he'd at least made sure his daughter had some tools when she left home. The problem, she quickly discovered, with fixing a few things was that you immediately became the flat's designated responsible person. 'Responsible' here meaning for everything.

Cress, for example, was a principled class warrior in the Socialist Workers Party. She was surprisingly able to reconcile this with her parents having bought her a Mini, just as she was with having grown up in West Hampstead, which she simply relabelled as Kilburn. She was a tireless advocate of working class rights except, it seemed, where it came to members of that class, such as Judy, having the right not to have to clear up after her. By the same token Toni, who was doing women's literature and gender studies, was committed to reversing the inequality inherent in women being allocated service and caring roles. Except when it came to expecting someone to serve and care for her.

How had it come about like this? Judy wondered. Had the pattern been set in the first year at university, when she'd shared halls of residence with them? Or did it begin earlier, in school or at home, where her downtrodden mother expected her to help clean up uncomplainingly after her father and underperforming brother? What was the invisible signal she gave off to people like Cress and Toni and Anne? Had someone pinned a sign that said 'doormat' on her back? And if she didn't somehow break the pattern now, was it going to be like this for the rest of her life? Was she, like the women who had once slept where she now slept, doomed to what seemed like an eternity of unremitting and inescapable obedience and servitude?

As Cress flapped around because she'd finally done her laundry and it had all come out of the machine pink, Judy worked on the phone, opening it up to examine its still well-preserved connections, neatly labelled in pencil over a century before, and working some newly bought beeswax into the wood. Cleaning the brass was hard work but she went at it like she was born to polish. It was worth it for the lovely archaic gleam she finally achieved. Its time in the attic had cost the Bakelite earpiece its sheen and on impulse she used a dab of metal polish on that too, finding that it restored it to its original glossy jet blackness.

She pressed it to her ear and heard. Heard? Time, nothingness, the sound of her own presence. A little like what she sensed as she hurried alone through the rest of the house on her way to and from the safety of their little flat.

It looked brilliant. She was proud of it, and of herself for finding and restoring it. Now, where to hang it?

She'd have liked to put it in her bedroom, but its walls were thin plasterboard. There were no communal rooms beyond the little bathroom and the ultra-compact kitchen. And their tiny landing hall, of course, which gave onto the narrow servants' staircase that would once have given the top floor's occupants their one bit of privacy and distance from the house they lived to serve.

It would have to be kitchen or hall, she decided. She didn't want to drill into tiles. A quick check online confirmed it. The phone was of a type that would have been found in large houses. There would have been a main telephone in the downstairs hall with a hand-crank for ringing the exchange and a simple button or pointer arrangement for making internal calls to extensions such as hers, which were typically installed in the servants' quarters, the study or sitting room and the stable, if there was one.

That would mean that their hall might very well have been where her phone had originally hung. She thought about it. From what she knew of a Victorian servant's life, it involved long days; rising in the cold of predawn to set the fires before their employers awoke, and working until night in a daylight-starved round of sweeping, blacking stoves, scrubbing grates and polishing cutlery, brass, silver and crystal, all the time being at the beck of the bell system that allowed the owners to summon you at any time from the kitchen or servants' dining room.

So why, she wondered, did they need a phone up here? Because, presumably, the maidservants were never off duty. Even when they climbed these stairs to fall into bed for a few hours sleep, they still had to be on call. Judy didn't accept Toni's certainty that a maid's life was one of near slavery until such time as she was inevitably thrown onto the streets pregnant with the master's child. Nor did she believe her descriptions of the Middle Ages as being entirely lit by bonfires made out of 'wise women' whose knowledge of ancient arts was eliminated in a vast holocaustal witch burning femicide carried out by a phallustocracy jealous of their knowledge. But she could well imagine it as a life of short nights, long days and freezing mornings. With the only reward your lodging and a stipend, plus fallen arches, varicose veins, hands cracked by cold water, and unceasing work until you were either, literally, an old maid, or married off to some callow butler's assistant. The latter not wholly different to the experiences of Judy's mother, who still went out to clean and scrub other people's houses in order to help pay for their own home, where she spent most of her waking moments doing the same.

She decided to wait till the others were out before fixing her phone in place, just in case Toni decided she wanted to hang one of her Monica Sjöö prints there, or Cress fancied it for an ironic statement involving a Ferrero Rocher party invitation, or a hook for her car keys.

Winter was coming and Judy was glad of the excuse to leave uni early and rush home before the park and its rain-wet, leaf-blown pavements surrendered entirely to darkness and the streetlamps' sodium yellow feebleness. She keyed open the huge front door, with its big brass knocker that had been made redundant by the rows of newly installed doorbells for the house's still empty flats. With only the fanlight to illuminate the huge tiled entrance hall everything was in shadow as she groped for the lights. Anyone could be hiding there, she felt, and with nobody else home she wasn't ashamed to run for the stairs and hurry up them before the timers on the light switches decided she'd had enough and plunged her into gloom.

She reached her front door and staircase and once again it felt the right place for her to be. Humble, fitting, modestly secure. A refuge from the echoing grandeur and implied demands of the rest of the building. There was no one home. Quickly she got ready the drill she'd borrowed specially from her dad.

There were three holes in the back of the phone for mounting it and it took little time to duplicate them on the wall and tap a rawlplug into each. It was difficult holding the phone in place with one hand while tightening the screws but she managed.

She stood back and admired it. It looked perfect. It was the kind of thing that no doubt Toni or Cress could have had any time they wanted when they were growing up, but not Judy, and it was her initiative that had got it for her now. She loved it. Better still, the spot she had chosen for it was just right. Anyone who saw it would think that it had always hung there. In fact, maybe it had.

She was putting the tools back in her room when she heard a key turn in the lock and Toni's footsteps on the stairs. Judy opened her door to point out what she'd done with the phone.

Which was when it began to ring.

Long slow rings, with a pregnant pause between, before the little hammer beat the bell into life again.

Judy stood, mouth opening. Toni looked from her to it, oblivious to the fact that it was an ornament, without electricity, unconnected to any telephone line.

"Nice one," she said, "you wired up that phone", then reached to answer it. Judy's "Don't!" was too faint for her to hear, or maybe it never even left her mouth at all.

Toni picked up the phone that couldn't be ringing. The bell stopped.

She put the microphone to her ear, but not so tightly that Judy couldn't hear, from far, far away, copper wire- and Bakelite-accented, the echoing susurration of a too-long held exhalation.

"It's for you," she said, and held out the earpiece to her.

"You're wanted downstairs."

WHAT'S BEHIND YOU?

Paul Finch

"I've never really experienced anything genuinely spooky or supernatural," Pendleton said. "With one exception."

The rest of us were all ears.

Pendleton was a dominant figure at the far end of the dining table. He was a tall, lean man with longish white hair, bright eyes, a sharp patrician nose and a square jaw. His blue velvet smoking jacket, frilled shirt and ruffled neck-cloth, far from making him look a dandy or eccentric, gave him an almost regal bearing. His clipped, resonant voice – despite his North Country background, he spoke perfect 'BBC English' – was entirely in keeping with his current role as Slade Professor of Fine Art at University College.

The wives in our small social group were particularly fascinated by him. He was the only one of us who was single, though he'd been married at least twice in the past. He drove a classic Daimler and lived in a large detached villa on the outskirts of Gerrards Cross, furnished with the utmost taste and style.

"Do tell us, Roy," Kirsty insisted, batting her spider-leg lashes at him. It was Halloween, and, with the exception of Pendleton, who always attended every function just as he was now, we'd dressed for dinner in accordance with the season. Kirsty was in 'Goth' persona: a high Pompadour wig dyed black, black eyeliner, black lipstick and a wraparound black silk dress. Her husband, Kevin, was more grotesquely clad in the bloodstained scrubs of a demented surgeon (somewhat disturbing, given that he was a surgeon by trade). I had come as Dracula in a black evening suit, a red-lined cape and white face makeup that was drying and cracking as the evening wore on. My actress wife, Liz, was decked as a sexy witch (I still can't work out when it was that Halloween witch-wear moved from stick-on warts and crooked carrot-noses to thigh boots, fishnet stockings and exposed décolletage). It was a similar story for the other two couples present: thoughtful combinations of horror chic and middle age sensuality. Of course, despite the time we'd taken attiring ourselves, as the evening had worn on much splendid food had gone down, good wine had flowed and we'd all become a little sated. Rounding things off by nibbling cheese, sipping cognac and airing a few ghost stories had seemed a splendid if somewhat traditional notion, though up until now Pendleton hadn't participated.

"Please do, Roy," Kirsty beseeched him, placing a hand complete with long, black-lacquered fingernails, on his arm. She wasn't flirting as such. Kirsty was a famous party-giver in our Buckinghamshire village, and treated all her guests with great attentiveness. "If this is something that's really happened, I'm sure we'd all be interested to hear it."

"Well ..." Pendleton shifted position in his chair. "I need you all to understand that I can't explain this event. It's just something that happened. It may have a rational explanation, but if so, I never discovered one. It concerns Sir James Ravenstock."

"The famous Welsh painter?" I said, surprised.

"The very same," Pendleton replied. He didn't seem surprised that I knew the man, but then I was a lecturer in social and economic history. Deciding that his audience was sufficiently rapt, Pendleton leaned forward, hands on the table, his long, slender fingers laced together. "Sir James was a close acquaintance of mine for several years, and is integral to this tale. Allow me to elaborate ..."

It was back in 1960. I was just seventeen years old, and on the Fine Arts course at the Wigan Art School, in Lancashire. It was a very well thought of establishment even in that rather depressed and industrialised part of England. Over the years we'd had some fairly illustrious names on the teaching staff – Lowry, Isherwood, Major. But the one in charge when I was a student there was Sir James Ravenstock.

It amazes me now, but at the time so many people took his presence on the faculty for granted, and yet he was a hugely successful artist, who had already produced an extensive and exquisite body of work. To this day, fifteen of his paintings are in the permanent collection at the Tate. He'd only come up north because he found the industrial landscapes an inspiration, much as he had done during his youth in his native South Wales. He was an excellent tutor, not just a good communicator but very thoughtful of his students. He was also a little set in his ways. He lived in a rural bungalow at the end of a rutted farm track, which you'd have been lucky to get a car along. This didn't trouble him as he didn't drive. He preferred to cycle everywhere, though this was less to do with physical fitness and more to do with his being a technophobe. He had no television or radio, though back in 1960 that wouldn't have been quite as startling as it would now.

His wife was significantly younger than he was, fair-haired and very pretty. Her name was Prunella. I understood that he'd first met her when she was modelling for him. We often used to nudge each other and express hope that she might someday come in and pose for us, but no such luck I'm afraid. Anyway, it was the end of the summer term that year, and at his own expense, Sir James had arranged for our class – seven of us in total – to travel down to the Gower Peninsula in West Wales, room in a comfortable boarding house at Rhossili Bay and take advantage of the wonderful summer light they get in that part of the world. Cornwall is very popular with painters because it boasts this incredible natural light, not to mention its epic seascapes and stunning coastal scenery. But the Gower boasts similar if not better, and is far less expensive.

Of course, back in those days West Wales was a long way from Lancashire. To get there we had to catch a train to Manchester, change at Cardiff, change to a bus at Swansea, by which time an entire day would have passed, and even then it was another hour's journey to Rhossili. As I recall, on the

87

morning in question we were all required to meet at Wigan Wallgate Station at some ungodly hour like six o'clock. Sir James had the furthest to travel to reach the railway station – he lived far out of town, and wasn't even close to a bus route. So I volunteered to assist. I was still living with my parents, and my father was a colliery deputy. He used to work what we in the north called 'the back shift', which meant that he finished around five o'clock in the morning. As such, it wasn't too inconvenient for him to give me a lift to the station at that early hour, and he agreed that en route we would divert out of town and collect Sir James from his house.

It was a glorious July morning, the sun already high and the birds twittering. But it was quite a surprise when we arrived at Sir James's bungalow, and found the front door closed and no sign of activity. I'd never been there before, and if I'm honest, the whole place was a little bit rundown. Sir James was not a bohemian type; he was quite dapper in public, so I was taken aback to see an untidy and overgrown front garden with elms and sycamores clumped tightly around the house, their branches literally lying across its roof. My father was more concerned about the state of his undercarriage after negotiating the tricky country lane; he now wondered gruffly why "the old dear" wasn't ready and waiting. He had no natural liking for the educational course I was pursuing, though thank God he never objected sufficiently to stop it. We waited, the Morris Minor chugging away, and still there was no sign of Sir James. It was very perplexing. My packed rucksack was stowed in the boot, along with my easel, my canvases, my brushes and boxes of paints. At the very least, I'd been expecting Sir James to be waiting at the front of his house with similar accoutrements. At length my father advised that I'd better go and "wake him up".

I climbed out, wandered up the path and knocked on the front door. There was no response; not even a sound from within. I walked around to the rear, which was also badly kept. The lawn had not been mown in some considerable time. There was such heavy underbrush down either side of it that it was difficult to see where the flowerbeds ended and the encroaching hedgerows began. The garden's far end was a mass of rank, interwoven weeds, which must have come to chest height, and this was where I finally spotted Sir James; he was emerging from these with hoe in hand – as if he'd been doing a spot of early-morning gardening. On seeing me, he approached along the lawn with a puzzled frown on his red, sweaty face. He was fully dressed, but his shirt and trousers were stained with leaf matter. His hair, normally neatly combed, hung in a mop of limp strands.

"My goodness, is it today?" he said, when I reminded him of our impending departure. "My goodness! I suppose I'd better get a move on."

"Is everything alright, Sir James?" I asked.

He nodded vigorously. "Yes, yes, absolutely. Do forgive me, erm ... Mr Pendleton. I knew we were going to Wales this week, but I must have lost track of the time."

It was a little bit worrying, I suppose – that a man should lose track of time to such an extent. But I was young. It never occurred to me that he might have some kind of problem. I doubt I'd even heard of words like 'dementia' or 'senility', and even if I had, I was so excited about going on holiday somewhere other than Blackpool that I gave it no real thought. Anyway, everything was soon resolved. Not five minutes later, Sir James appeared at the front of the house, valise and silver-headed cane in hand, wearing a shoulder-caped greatcoat and hat (he always wore this rather flamboyant fedora, which, he being such a short man, looked ridiculous on him, though we never dared to say anything). He thanked us profusely as I opened the rear passenger door for him. My father nodded and smiled tolerantly. Just before I climbed in, I glanced up and saw Sir James's wife watching us from an upper window. She was half-concealed by the curtain, which was a good thing as she only appeared to be wearing a wrap of some sort, but she cut a lonely, rather forlorn figure. It struck me, and not for the first time, that marriage to someone significantly older than oneself was always likely to be fraught with problems.

Not that this lingered in my mind for very long. After all, we were now embarked on our much-anticipated holiday, though of course we still had a monumentally long and boring train journey ahead of us. The early stages of this were enlivened by one of the other chaps, the name of Gibbon, who'd picked up a paperback from a newspaper stand on the station platform. It was the now-famous *Pan Book of Horror Stories*, which at the time had just been published, and he entertained us all by reading from it aloud, though eventually his throat became sore and he insisted on taking a break. We'd been travelling for what seemed hours by now, and were crossing the rolling summits of central Wales, stopping at mountain halts so remote that I'm sure only shepherds ever used them. Even though the Pan book was closed, we continued to discuss the odd and ghostly. A rather delicate young fellow – his name was Flickwood, he spoke with a lisp and had the most ludicrous 'basin' haircut you've ever seen – mentioned a legend we were all reasonably familiar with about a spectre that roamed the warren of underground galleries linking our home town's coal mines. His father and grandfather, both colliers, supposedly knew men who had seen and heard it. We presumed there would be similar ghosts in the Welsh coal mining areas. And that was when Sir James, who had slept most of the way and paid scant attention to Gibbon's recitations, suddenly interjected with: "Gentlemen, I assure you there is no ghost quite like the one in the old Rectory at Rhossili Bay."

Obviously we wanted to know more.

"There have been shipwrecks on that coast throughout history," he said in his melodious Welsh voice. "And it's entirely possible the injured and dying were brought ashore at Rhossili Bay and perhaps spent their final minutes in Rhossili Rectory, a remote structure at the foot of Rhossili Down, and at one time the only habitation in the vicinity. There were also stories that this Rectory was built on the site of a Dark Age monastery, sacked by the Danes and later buried in sand during a tempest."

I remember that he watched us all closely as he spoke, smiling like a cat. He had a thick, red-grey brush of a beard and moustache, and round spectacles. His eyes, which were very green, twinkled like jewels beneath the rim of his fedora.

"However," he added ominously, "none of these potentially dramatic events can really explain the true depths of fear and despair this unholy presence has caused. You see, gentlemen … you must never turn and look. That is what they say." We exchanged baffled glances, and he chuckled in that hearty way of his. "Rhossili Rectory is now ruined and empty, and according to the story an evil spirit haunts it. One can only surmise that it may be connected to the historical events I have mentioned. But whatever its origins, the locals don't take this as a joke. You'll notice that when we arrive. The Rectory is far along the beach from Rhossili village and the boarding house where we'll be staying. It's very isolated – people do *not* go there."

"What form does this spirit take?" Flickwood asked, sounding nervous.

"Oh, Mr Flickwood … you walk through that ruined building on your own, day or night, and you will find out. I guarantee it."

I recall my hair creeping at the base of my neck as Sir James said this. Admittedly he was an artist, he was the sort of person given to flights of fancy, but he told us with such intensity, his cat-green eyes fixed on us through the lenses of his spectacles, that I really got the impression he was telling us something he believed to be true.

"You won't see it," he added. "But you will hear it. For it will whisper in your ear … *What's behind you?*" He sang that last sentence in a musical baritone. "*What's … behind … you?*"

We were riveted. The only other sound was the dull, regular thud of the sleepers as the train trundled through the Welsh high country. Beyond the windows, low cloud spilled though a range of craggy, tooth-like peaks.

"What's behind you?" Sir James said again. "And whatever you do, boyo … on no account turn and look."

"But if you do, what will you see?" Flickwood asked in a near-whisper.

Sir James smiled. "That's the point … it's something supposedly so dreadful that it will affect you for the rest of your days."

"Has anyone ever looked?" I enquired.

He mused. "The story goes that one or two have been bold enough, but that whatever they saw left its mark upon them. They were quiet men from that point, who rarely spoke. All the joy of life had gone out of them. They refused ever to say what it was they had seen, though one did give the warning: 'Never look back. Not if you value your sanity.'"

For the most part – and remember, this was a less sophisticated era – we'd been raised as children on a diet of simplistic ghost stories featuring sheet-covered figures with rattling chains. This was so different from anything of that sort that it genuinely unnerved us. When we finally reached Rhossili Bay late in the evening, one of the first things we looked out for, despite our excitement at having arrived, was the Rectory.

Pendleton paused to take a sip of cognac.

"That old Rectory has now been refurbished and is a holiday let, I'm led to believe," he said. "I wouldn't know whether it's still supposed to be haunted. I've never been near the place since these events occurred, and I'll never go there again in the future."

"Something happened then?" Kirsty asked eagerly.

"Oh yes." He nodded solemnly. "Something happened."

Rhossili Bay is one of the loveliest places you are ever likely to visit on the British coast. The beach is white as talcum powder, and curves inward along the shoreline in a slow, graceful, three-mile crescent. Back in 1960 it was completely unspoiled, strewn only with shells and dried seaweed, broken here and there by the wizened timbers of wrecks jutting up from the pristine sand like the ribs of ancient saurians. It is hemmed to the sea – that blue, foaming, ever-roaring Atlantic – by high Rhossili Down, a rolling green cliff-top crowned with gorse, and the site of both Bronze Age and Viking burial mounds. Worm's Head islet, the bay's snaking, rocky headland, is famous for the seals that brazenly sun themselves there.

We were staying in a boarding house in Rhossili village at the south end of the bay. This was run by a friendly dragon called Mrs Devereux, who, while she was hugely demanding in terms of the condition we left our rooms in each morning – two bunks to each one as I recollect, so we had to work to stay on top of the mess – she also provided hearty breakfasts of bacon, eggs and sausage on toast, basic but satisfying dinners in the evening – pie, chips, beans and so forth, and if we were prepared to pay extra, packed lunches for during the day. We didn't always take the latter option. Sometimes we ate fish and chips at lunchtime, or were able to buy sandwiches from one of several coastal hostelries, rather marvellous places actually, their exteriors weatherboarded and crusted with salt, their interiors decked with nautical memorabilia: nets, anchors, harpoons, oilskins. Several times in the evening we repaired to one of these welcoming establishments and, even at that tender age, managed to work our way through a few pints of good crisp ale. I'm mainly a wine drinker these days, but there was something thoroughly heartwarming about settling down in the nook of a pub after an invigorating day in the fresh air, and treating yourself to a measure of rich red beer with a cap of white froth – especially when you'd only forked out tuppence for it.

But of course this wasn't the purpose of our visit. We were there to paint, which an entire week of benign weather only encouraged. Some of us set up our easels on the cliff-tops, from where the vista was astounding. Others preferred the beach, where they could get close to the water's edge. There were various items of interest down there: as I say, the bones of desiccated wrecks and the seals lolling on Worm's Head; but also Portuguese men-o-war, a large species of Atlantic jellyfish, lying marooned all over the sand like great puddles of translucent slime. And then of course, Rhossili Rectory.

This was located on a low but natural plateau far back from the beach itself and tucked into the foot of the Down, about half way between Rhossili and the next village along, Llangennith. I mentioned that we'd all been fascinated to note it on our first day, but as the business of the holiday had got underway we'd put it to the backs of our minds. It was still there, however, lowering on the edge of our awareness. I find it difficult to describe the place now. From a distance it didn't look particularly dilapidated. It was just a large, four-sided house, but there was no glass in any of its windows and all that remained of its doorways were frames. If there'd ever been a garden around it, it was now deeply overrun with briars, thistles and other thorny scrub. At one point during the week, we passed it closely while looking for a path leading up to the Down, and were assailed by that unpleasant damp smell you often get around derelict houses – like stale urine. We saw bare joists showing where slates were missing from its roof. The sea breeze groaned through it. I remember a loose piece of guttering tapping relentlessly against the eaves – as if some invisible hand were manipulating it. One evening, possibly the Wednesday, when we passed it by overhead walking along the cliff-top path, we dared each other to venture down there. Sir James, who'd been more jovial that week than I could ever remember – moving each day from one work-in-progress to the next, offering suggestions and solutions, teaching "on the hoof" as he called it, but in easy, affable fashion – suddenly looked stern and overruled any such foolishness, pointing out that someone attempting to find his way down there at night would likely break a leg, or maybe worse.

However, he then became thoughtful and added: "Perhaps we'll go down there on our last morning, and see if any of you can actually meet the challenge of Rhossili Rectory without first needing to fuel yourself with courage of the Dutch variety."

This became our unofficial plan for the end of the week: on our last morning, before boarding our bus, which was due to leave Rhossili village at 9.30 a.m., we would pack up and make a last visit to the beach, to see if anyone was brave enough to walk through the Rectory on his own. Not everyone was happy about this: Flickwood for one, who after agonising in silence for a whole day, finally admitted that he wasn't going to do it because just worrying about it would ruin what remained of his week. The rest of us weren't unduly concerned as this meant Flickwood could wait at the village car park, where the bus was due to arrive, and look after our bags. But I don't think anyone was hugely enthused by what we'd agreed to do – especially not when that final morning arrived. We were all in that slightly giddy state when you feel you've had a worthwhile holiday and are looking forward to going home and resuming normal life. In fact, if anything, going down to the Rectory now seemed like an inconvenience. We'd had a good old drink and singsong in the pub the night before, and most of us were simply happy to sit on the car park wall, waiting for the bus. But oddly, it was Sir James who now seemed most interested in the Rectory.

"Well gentlemen," he said consulting his pocket watch. "We have fifty minutes. Time enough to investigate the mysteries of the universe."

It was the first grey day we'd had, and windy. Ripples passed through the marram grass lying to either side of the cliff path as we dutifully descended in single file. Twists of blown sand scuttled across the beach below. The slate-tinged sea crashed and boomed, throwing up fountains of spume. I was at the rear with only Sir James behind me, and when we got down to the bottom and trekked along the beach, he remained in that position, muttering under his breath. At first I barely noticed – the closer we drew towards that distant, solitary structure, the more apprehensive I was feeling. I had that absurd but familiar sensation that my only escape route, the path to the cliff-top, was falling further and further behind me. Only after several seconds of these ruminations did I realise that Sir James wasn't muttering to himself, he was talking to *me* – albeit quietly.

"That's what we're about today, Mr Pendleton ... the universe. One has a duty to glance into the great beyond if one has the chance. One must always seek to answer the unanswerable questions."

"I don't know about that, Sir James," I said, glancing around. He wasn't looking at me. His eyes were fixed on the old building as it loomed closer. "I was wondering if we ... well, if we've actually got time for this. Suppose the bus comes early?"

He either didn't hear this, or was so absorbed in his own thoughts that he failed to detect any anxiety on my part. "There are times in every man's life when he must take a leap into the dark, if nothing else to reassure himself that the darkness doesn't go on indefinitely."

I tried to laugh. "But we're not doing that today, are we? I mean this is just a game, isn't it? A little joke?"

Abruptly, he seemed to wake. "A joke, of course." He nodded robustly. "But what a wonderful way to round off an exhilarating week, wouldn't you agree?"

I couldn't actually have agreed less. But it would have seemed churlish to dispute with him when he was clearly so keen. He was stiff-shouldered, almost ramrod straight, as we followed a path up from the sand onto the plateau, which was knee-deep in a thick, furze-like grass. The rim of Sir James's fedora flapped backward in the breeze as we marched along it. His eyes were still fixed on the approaching ruin, bright and flat as coins.

Close up, the Rectory seemed larger than it had before,

which suggested that 'walking through it' as Sir James had said, wouldn't necessarily be quick or easy. It must have had three floors, and probably a cellar area as well, and there'd be multiple rooms on each level. It might have been comforting to see gulls perched along the edges of its steeply angled roofs, of which there were several, or among its numerous misaligned chimney pots, but strangely – given that it was summer – there was no sign of life at all. It was even more disconcerting to note that what I'd thought were empty window frames contained closed timber shutters, though all had rotted black thanks to the damp sea-wind. The front door was also firmly closed, crisscrossed with a higgledy-piggledy mass of planks, which looked as if they had been nailed there swiftly rather than carefully. Every other aspect of the house was as odious as you'd expect for a structure abandoned for so long: its walls were of weathered red brick and coated with fungus-like moss. Its eaves hung with threads of shrivelled brown ivy. All its pipework was rusted and broken. Fallen slates scattered the cement paths leading around either side of it.

After some muted debate, we took the path on the left. This led us through to a side garden, though it was actually more like a jungle of semi-decayed foliage, which rose far over our heads. There was an open entrance to the house on this side: a low doorway, which at first looked as if it was only about three feet tall, but then we approached and saw that it stood at the base of a flight of cellar steps. Clearly there had once been a solid door fitted there – both its jambs had perished but they were also splintered, as if someone had forced entry. Thrill-seekers like ourselves, I supposed. Beyond this entrance lay only skulking darkness.

We stood there, the hair prickling our scalps. I know it sounds like a cliché, but the notion that we were being observed was overpowering. We glanced constantly over our shoulders, but the dense green tangle that shrouded us masked any sight of the beach or the rolling surf. The distant explosions of the waves were only just audible.

Gibbon cleared his throat. "What are we … erm, what're we supposed to do now that we're here, Sir James?"

"Hmmm!" Sir James leaned on his cane. "As I understand it, there are no set rules. Except that … well, you walk through from one side to the other."

"Is there an open door on the other side?" I asked.

He shrugged as he gazed into the unlit recess. "I imagine there must be. Someone's broken this one open. Almost certainly they'll have broken one on the other side."

Almost certainly. Two simple words, yet they conveyed far more menace than they had any right to. Almost certainly – but perhaps not? And who would be the first one to discover that he'd wandered into what was actually a cul-de-sac, with some sinister presence close behind him?

"Who goes first?" Sir James asked, so sharply that we all jumped. In retrospect it seems ridiculous to have been so frightened. The house was larger than we'd thought, but if one were to dash through it, he'd be out the other side in less than twenty seconds – assuming he could find a clear route. And yet still no one volunteered, though Sir James had apparently anticipated this. He produced a fistful of fresh-cut grass stems, and said we were to draw one each.

How inevitable was it, I wonder, that the one I selected would have another one tied to the end of it? I remember peering at it with some vague feeling that life was a conspiracy.

"Go ahead, Mr Pendleton," Sir James said in a faux grave tone. He regarded me with something like a fond smile, but his eyes were hard and shiny, as if they would brook no refusal. "Let's see some of this famous northern grit, shall we?"

The others were watching me, white-faced, so I tried to make light of it, shrugging, pretending it would be all in a morning's work – though inwardly I had this dull, almost numbing consciousness that my ordeal had now begun and was irreversible.

I descended the cellar steps stealthily, but still imagining the reports of my footfalls echoing ahead of me through the eerie structure, certain to disturb anything that wasn't already disturbed.

"Remember," Sir James said from behind – he and the others already felt a significant distance away, "on no account, turn back and look."

I repeated this to myself over and over, as I strode forward into the blackness, hands groping out ahead of me. No looking back. No looking back. Whatever happened, whatever I heard, I would not look back. My intent was simply to bullock my way through, blinded by darkness or not, keeping going with my head down until I was out the other side. But immediately I saw that it wouldn't be this simple. No sooner had I entered that first underground chamber than the dull grey daylight started to penetrate past me, revealing a bare brick corridor, whitewashed sometime in the past but now festooned with cobwebs and densely cluttered with items of broken furniture – tables, chairs and stools, several covered in mildewed rags or stacked with wooden crates. There was even a row of coat pegs on one of the walls, with an old canvas coat hanging from one of them. I tried to ignore this as I negotiated my way past, though I now kept replaying in my head a scene from some silent comedy I'd watched – Buster Keaton or Harry Langdon – in which a hanging coat is left to its own devices, only for a pair of feet to appear at the bottom, gloved hands to emerge from the sleeve cuffs and a cowled head to appear above the collar, the coat then detaching itself from the hanger and creeping furtively after the hero and heroine.

I glanced back several times at the coat, just for reassurance that it was still hanging there innocently – only to remind myself in a moment of shock insight that was something like a dash of cold water, that I should not be looking behind me at all!

Only now did it strike me how much of a challenge this was going to be – never looking back as I slowly, cautiously progressed. But was it the case that I was *never* supposed to look back, or did it only apply when or if I heard the voice? I was still debating this with myself when I reached the end of the cellar corridor, where there was a T-junction – two opposing passages heading off into noisome darkness, and a stone switchback stair with a rusty handrail leading upward. Here, I loitered haplessly. Again, that foetid 'empty house' stench was ripe. I didn't want to go upstairs – if there was no exit from up there, that would be quite a detour; but neither did I want to venture along either of the next two passages. There was no glimmer of light from them, and the stench seemed even thicker. The more I pondered it, the less likely it seemed that there would be another door on the cellar level.

I glanced upward, and saw a faint silver radiance, no doubt a combination of numerous chinks of daylight filtering around shutters or through the gaps between heavy, dust-thick drapes – certainly no guarantee that my escape route lay that way. But, with no real choice, I ascended slowly, again stepping as lightly as I could. It was impossible not to picture the labyrinthine spaces above me – more rooms, more corridors, all dusty and empty, save maybe for similar relics of furniture to those I'd seen below. Perhaps some of these would be nothing more in the gloom than large, eerily shaped objects covered with sheets, and I would have to sidle narrowly past them. I was suddenly desperate to be back outside with the others, or in the village car park sitting on the wall with Flickwood, even if he did have a basin crop – at least the air would be fresh and there'd be a human presence on all sides of me. But still I ascended, thrusting these ideas aside. It was just a derelict house, I told myself. That was all there was to it.

At the top of the stair I entered the entry hallway. I could see more clearly in here because though the front door, which was about thirty yards away, was blocked from the other side, there was a fanlight over the top of it – it was covered by a stained sheet, though this admitted a muted glow. I could see enough to distinguish that the parquet floor was covered with leaves, and that there were several dark doorways on either side of it. I turned my gaze from one to the next. The room I sought would most likely be the kitchen, but behind which portal did it lie?

The first led me into an old lounge area, now a gutted shell. Bare boards lay where there had once been a carpet, and the paper on the walls hung only in strips as if someone had been vigorously rending at it; looking closely, the few strips remaining appeared to have been shredded by the claws of an animal. But my biggest shock came after my eyes had attuned properly to the dimness and I turned to the large fireplace, and noted a bath-chair to one side – with what looked like a figure reposed in it.

The impression was so lifelike that I almost turned and fled, though somehow I resisted this and edged a little closer, eyes goggling – before it struck me that the chair contained nothing but a bundle of blankets. Even then I wasn't completely put at ease. The blankets, which were exceedingly old and dirty, had been dumped in the bath-chair rather than folded and placed there neatly. As such, the corner of one musty old quilt had risen up at the point where a human head would be and drooped forward a little, creating what looked like a peaked hood. It was difficult to believe there'd be sufficient space under there to conceal a human. But even so, I found myself crouching and peeking warily in, half expecting to see some hideous, mouldering visage. Strangely, the empty hollow I saw instead was even more unsettling.

I straightened up, reminding myself that it wasn't my purpose to investigate this house, merely to pass through it. Clearly there was to be no exit via this room, nor in the next, which might have been an old dining area. In some ways, the murky half-light in these chambers was actually worse than full darkness would have been. I could make out pale oblongs on the walls where pictures had once hung, broken figurines on mantelpieces, fireplaces where the grates were stuffed with old newspapers and feathers. Everything was grimy, dingy and damp – in short, dead. And yet it was easy to imagine that my presence here had invoked a kind of hostility. I was just passing through a pair of double doors into a morning room of sorts, when I stopped cold.

That sounds so melodramatic, I now realise – but at the time I literally froze, listening as intently as I could, my heart pounding.

From one of the other rooms, almost certainly the lounge, had come the sound of wheels creaking. Only slightly – a couple of metallic squeaks and then silence again, but I was in no doubt that I had just heard the bath-chair moving.

Before I knew what I was doing – again ignoring the vital instruction "don't look back" – I'd stridden out of the morning room, back along the hall and into the lounge. I'm not sure where this temporary courage came from. Possibly I was expecting that one of the other chaps had sneaked into the house after me and was playing games, even though I felt certain that Sir James had come here with a much higher purpose. Once I was back in the lounge, I was almost disappointed to find it exactly as I'd left it. There was nobody else in there, just the dimness and the dust. The bath-chair might have moved from its original position, but if so it was infinitesimal. It remained motionless as I stared at it. And then I noted something different about it – the raised 'hood' had collapsed forward. Which suggested that, infinitesimal or not, there had been *some* movement.

I hurried on my way, determined to get the ordeal over as quickly as possible. I crossed back through the morning room and along a very dark corridor towards what simply must be the kitchen. But now I had to pass the foot of the main staircase, which, rather unconventionally, was located in an entirely enclosed stairwell, the black entrance to which sat at a facing angle to the kitchen door. I paused before passing it. It seemed too likely that someone – a friend thinking of playing a joke, or maybe some dangerous vagabond – could be lurking in there just waiting to jump out on me.

I cast around to try and provide myself with a weapon, but nothing came to hand. Deciding that delay was only protracting the torture, I bunched my fists and went boldly forward, passing the stairwell entrance without even glancing into it, and turning into the kitchen, which had been fitted in 'naval galley' fashion in that it was long and narrow with worktops down either side. It was in a filthy state; everything aged and decayed, fallen tiles exposing bare brick walls. But a door stood open a crack at the far end, and daylight glimmered around it.

Relieved, I hurried down there, yanking the door open – only to find that I was in a concrete annexe comprising three more rooms. The first, to my left, looked like a scullery, as three sides were fitted with deep, empty shelves. The second, directly in front of me, looked like a utilities passage – it was filled with shattered masonry and flooded to a depth of maybe an inch; all types of rusted, sawn-off plumbing jutted from the rotted plaster crumbling from its walls. Thirdly, to my right, was what appeared to be a coal room, little more now than a bare stone chamber, and it was from in here, thanks to a high letterbox-shaped window of frosted glass, that the light was issuing.

"*What's behind you?*" the voice whispered in my ear.

I'd just been pondering the improbability of there being no rear door to this house, when I realised that I had been spoken to. It's quite incredible how, despite all the warning advice you've been given to never look round, that first moment you feel certain someone has stepped up behind you, your immediate instinct is to spin and confront them. And I was so close to doing just that.

Good Lord, only some sixth sense prevented me!

I froze again, beset by a terror that words can barely describe. There was no question in my mind about this being one of the others fooling with me, for the voice had not come from earthly vocal cords. It had drifted into my hearing range with a sibilance born of wind, ice, dust, emptiness, despair. It was overwhelming, that sense – that something more awful than I could possibly imagine was immediately behind me, and that I only needed to turn my head slightly, and – but no!

Even if I'd been of a mind to, I couldn't have turned.

With my body making some bizarre rebellion in the name of good sense, certain of my muscles and joints appeared to lock. I was facing away from whatever it was – into the dank, three-way cul-de-sac, and that was the only way I would be permitted to go. And slowly now, as my eyes attuned to this next level of dimness, I saw that at the far end of the utilities passage, where I'd thought there was only a brick wall, there was a door with a latch and bar.

Stiffly, like some automaton, I lumbered towards it.

I could still sense that nebulous presence behind me, following close, whispering again: "*What's behind you … ?*"

It was barely audible and yet I heard it clear as day as I splashed my way forward through the mass of broken pipes and fallen plaster, and then I was at the property's rear door. I don't know what I'd have done had I found that bar jammed fast – possibly had a heart attack – but it wasn't. It moved almost smoothly, as if oiled. There was a *clank* and *bang* as I struck the latch, and the door swung open.

Merciful Heaven, full daylight and clean air embraced me.

I tottered forward like a drunk, though my ordeal wasn't entirely over. A crazy-paved path wound ahead of me, hedged from either side by tall, densely matted vegetation. As I stumbled along it, I could still sense something to my rear, pursuing me every inch of the way, taunting me, tempting me to look around. A scream of panic was trapped in my chest, ready to burst out at a second's notice, but I suppressed it and kept on walking until at last I was away from the wretched property and striding through knee-deep furze, the soles of my shoes breaking a crust of sandy loam beneath. I can't tell you what a joy it was to see the Down rising to my left and the roaring seascape on my right, and at that very same moment to realise that I was alone again – that I was back in the normal world. I sank to my knees as if I'd just run a marathon, wringing with sweat, and only finally glanced up and back towards the house, now concealed from me by the vegetation clinging around it, when, maybe five minutes later, I heard the voice of Gibbon, who had clearly been selected to follow me through next.

"You alright?" he said, approaching, eyeing me curiously. "Bit rum in there, bit grubby and all. But nothing to get excited about, I don't think."

"You …" I stammered, "you didn't hear anything?"

"Not at all." He was blank-faced. "Did you?"

"No," I lied. At least I think I lied. Already I was having doubts. Had my overactive imagination foxed me inside that dingy, stagnant house, every aspect of which had seemed custom-made for the frightful fantasy bestowed on it?

One by one, the other chaps emerged. Most looked relieved to have made it through. A fellow called Barton was grumbling because he'd completely lost his way in the gloom and had bashed his knee on something. But he was sweating hard, which suggested that he'd probably charged through at full pelt, which also explained his injury. None wore the harrowed mask that must have been on my face when I'd emerged – none until Sir James came through, right at the end. When he swayed into view, I saw an expression that almost stopped my breath. His teeth were bared but locked together so tightly there were deep, scimitar-like furrows at either end of his mouth. His green eyes were fixed like Christmas baubles, staring directly ahead but glazed as though he was only semi-conscious. His skin was the colour of chalk.

"Did … you see something?" I asked,

"I … erm, hah!" he replied, coming round and grinning at us, though his eyes remained glassy. "Of course not. Nothing at all. There's nothing to see, is there?"

"Did you *hear* it though?" one of the other boys asked.

Sir James now made a great show of being unperturbed by his walk through the Rectory. "The whole thing's just a silly legend," he boomed. "Something for the tourists, which is exactly what we are, boyos. Though if we don't get a move on, we'll become residents, because our bus leaves in the next fifteen minutes."

I couldn't help noticing that he didn't say anything else after that, at least not until we were on the bus and en route back to Swansea. And when we arrived in Swansea, and had to walk to the railway station, he stopped and made a lengthy call from a public payphone. "Remiss of me," he muttered afterwards. "First time I've called home all week."

Of course, when it comes to holidays, the long homeward journey tends to be a bit more of a drag than the long outward one. As a group we had plenty to talk about, though it was interesting that no one really mentioned the Rectory and that there were no more *Pan Horror* stories. Sir James conversed barely at all during this stage of the trip, but instead sat alone and appeared to be sketching something on a sheet of paper. When I tried to glance over his shoulder, he moved it away from me.

"No peeking, Mr Pendleton," he said sternly.

"Will this be your next masterpiece?" I asked.

"Possibly the greatest of them all," he replied. He noticed that the others had taken interest, and, with a melodramatic sigh, folded the sheet, inserted it into an envelope and slid it into his inside pocket. "Can't a true artist ever have a little privacy?" he complained.

Midway along that laborious stretch of line between Cardiff and Manchester, the chirpy conversations dried up in favour of quiet contemplation and ultimately, as we had the compartment to ourselves, more singing. Everyone had a go. I chipped in with 'Living Doll', which went down rather well, especially as two of the other chaps accompanied me by performing the Hank Marvin and Bruce Welch two-step. Sir James laughed until I thought his sides would break. But pride of place went to his own recitation: a quite marvellous, full-length version of 'Land Of My Fathers', a hymn, which, even if you're English, always has the power to bring a tear to the eye.

It was late evening when we changed trains at Manchester,

and summer dusk was falling. Another forty minutes later, and we disembarked at Wigan Wallgate, where it was now completely dark. There were several people on the lamp-lit platform; mostly these were our parents waiting to meet us, but there were also several men in uniform, and two in trench coats. It was one of the latter who approached us.

"James Ravenstock?" he said.

"That's correct, sir," Sir James replied, straightening his lapels.

"I'm Detective Sergeant Cranwood, and I must ask you to come with me."

Sir James nodded soberly. "Of course. You looked where I directed you?"

The rest of us stood watching in confused surprise, though I now recalled the lengthy phone call Sir James had made from Swansea bus station.

"We did, sir," Cranwood replied, and he took hold of Sir James by the wrist. In my naïve way I tried to intervene, but one of the uniformed officers held me back.

"You've got the wrong man!" I shouted. "Sir James has done nothing wrong."

"Your faith in me in inspiring, Mr Pendleton," Sir James replied. "I'm also flattered that you found that portrait of my wife, the one in the upper window, so lifelike."

"But that was ..." The words died on my tongue.

"Take charge of this, if you would," Sir James said. They were now applying handcuffs to his wrists, but first he had time to slip me the envelope containing the folded sheet on which he'd sketched. "Feel free to examine it, though I advise against it."

I was still aghast by what was happening. Everyone was. No one could understand it, but now I gazed down at the envelope in my hand, and a secondary shock jolted through me as I realised what the sketch inside it depicted.

"*You looked back,*" I said to him. "*You heard the voice and you looked back.*"

He smiled sadly. "Whether I'd looked or not, it clearly would have made no difference. But once I *had* looked, I saw no point in delaying matters." Sir James assumed an air of studied dignity as they prepared to lead him away. "It's been a pleasure, gentlemen. You are all fellows of the highest calibre."

Pendleton lowered his head, deep in thought.

"Did you look at the sketch?" I finally ventured.

He glanced up. "I did indeed. It had a profound impact on me. So much that I can only thank Heaven I never looked around when the voice was calling to me."

"But what did he see?" Kirsty asked, fascinated.

In response, Pendleton removed from his inside pocket an old, brown-edged envelope. There were gasps around the table as he slid out the crinkled sheet from within and unfolded it. "Hardly his best work," he said. "But then it was only a preliminary sketch."

We gazed, appalled – at the image of a stick-man dangling from a stick-gallows.

BEN'S BEST FRIEND

Gary Power

Ben had a new best friend, Andy. Andy had moved down from Liverpool. They met at the local rec'; they'd become mates straight away. Andy swore a lot and that made him laugh. It was always "fucking this" and "fucking that". Ben went home one day and said, "Is my fucking tea ready?" 'cause Andy dared him. His dad clipped him around his ear and sent him to bed early.

Andy's dad imported exotic animals. Sometimes he kept them at their house – that was what Andy said. Ben had never seen them. He'd heard them though.

They sounded scary.

Ben always left Andy's religiously at 10.30 p.m. so that he'd be home by eleven. The first part of his journey, a half-mile cycle ride down the Fairway took him out of the Bay Estate. The Bay Estate was a sort of council estate for the filthy rich. There were fifteen lampposts; Ben knew because he counted them every time. He'd reach the exit to the estate and then turn back so that he could watch the lights go out. They went out one by one, starting with the furthest. The estate would slowly be plunged into total darkness. It gave Ben the creeps, but in a thrilling way. In his imagination, when it got dark, the Bay Estate became a bleak and savage world inhabited by flesh-eating creatures.

Sometimes he'd be a few minutes late and the lights would go out as he cycled down the Fairway. That was even better. The darkness would chase him and his heart would race. He'd be shit-scared but at the same time excited. The flesh-eaters would be tearing after him but as long as he was in the light, he was safe.

Then one day he left even later than usual. It was Andy's fault. His parents were out for the night. They raided the drinks cabinet, got drunk on cheap sherry and amused themselves by making a few funny phone calls. Ben became anxious when he realised the time, but that added to the excitement.

It was 10.45 p.m.

He'd *never* been that late before.

The streetlights were still on when he left and that set his pulse racing.

He reckoned he could make it though. The first light went out behind him. Ben raised himself from the saddle and pushed down hard on the peddles. A quick glance over his shoulder and he saw that three, maybe four streetlights had gone out. The fear was irrational, but his imagination was working overtime. He wasn't on a bike he was on a Harley. He'd made halfway when a flood of darkness passed him. His blood ran cold. His pulse raced. He laughed – nervously. The feel of cold air rushing by felt good.

And then he saw four figures silhouetted across the exit to the estate as if they were waiting for him.

And that made him stop.

"Fuck ..." he said.

His blood ran cold. When he looked again one of them was gone. The remaining three things were making horrible sounds – like grunting through thick phlegm. They began to walk in his direction. Not really a walk, more of a demented swagger.

"Oh fucking shit ..." he groaned.

Ben thought he might piss himself. He doubted that they could see him. He was in darkness. Silently he moved from the road, abandoned his bike and slipped into the front garden of one of the big houses. He'd hide until they'd gone and then make a dash for it. Peeping through a leylandii hedge, he watched them. They were looking in gardens and down drives. Ben thought he could smell something horrible, like the filthy stench from a sewer.

He moved further back into the cover of the trees. There was enough moonlight for him to see the closest one. It had a jutting jaw and wild, bulbous eyes. It had pustulent skin and clumps of hair missing like it had radiation sickness. It was naked – that really freaked him. By the look of its stonking great genitalia, it was male.

Ben felt sick.

He was either going to puke or piss himself. For a moment the thing looked in his direction. He shrank back into the shadows. His breathing was slow and shallow. The beast pulled a strange face; it was sniffing the air. It could probably smell him. He wanted to cry. He wanted to be home. He wanted to be tucked up in bed.

Warm, cosy and safe.

The sudden sound of frenzied laughter filled the air and it was coming from his pocket. It was his stupid fucking ring tone.

Andy was texting him.

U hme yet m8? A.

His cover was blown. The closest one moved like lightning and dragged him through the hedge by his hair. They were hideous things. The other two were female. They had droopy, hairy breasts from which protruded stumpy nipples. One of them let out a hellhound shriek; the sound cut through him like a knife. They had clawed hands and teeth like razors.

They started tearing at his clothes.

"What are you doing?" he screamed. "What are you fucking doing?"

His bladder went into spasm and he felt the warm flow of urine running down his leg. The fourth one stepped from the shadows but it wasn't a beast.

It was human.

Ben couldn't believe his eyes.

"Andy?" he said.

The skin of a young boy was found hanging in a tree on the Fairway to the Bay Estate early the next morning. There were a few bits of raw flesh on the ground. Forensics found hair, fingernails and some teeth. They found an eyeball in a nearby drain as well. The other one had rolled down the road, but a young PC called Colin accidentally trod on it.

There was no evidence though so they stitched up a known paedo who lived on the estate just to keep the public happy.

Andy cycled down the Fairway a few days later. He was mourning the loss of his best mate. There was some consolation though. He had a new bike – not exactly new, sort of ... refurbished.

He was off to the rec' to find a new best friend.

THE THINGS THAT AREN'T THERE

Thana Niveau

I'm not good with kids. I told Mrs Pearce this but she said not to be silly, that everyone loved children, especially girls like me who would be mummies too someday.

"Not me," I said, making a face.

"Nonsense, Emma! You're only twelve. Believe me, you'll feel differently when you're older."

"No I won't."

The year before, my mother had shown me the video of my own birth. But the magical, beautiful event I'd been promised was more like a nightmare. I couldn't believe the wild-eyed screaming woman was my mother and I *refused* to believe that the bloody, slimy thing that split her open down there was me. The room started to spin and then I was sick all down the front of my new jumper.

"I'm *never* having kids," I said, swallowing the horrible memory.

"Oh, you just wait and see." Mrs Pearce ruffled my hair and smiled the way grown-ups do when they think they know everything. Then she went right back to telling me all I needed to know about watching Chloe while she was out.

I grumbled and said okay I would but that I hadn't wanted to do babysitting at all and Chloe could be really annoying and it was only because my parents had *made* me …

I didn't really say any of that. I just thought it at her really hard. Maybe if I made her feel guilty enough she'd never ask me again.

"It's only for a couple of hours," she said, as though she'd simply asked me to post a letter for her, "and you know how Chloe looks up to you."

Did I ever. Chloe was the most annoying kid in the world. The whiny six-year-old got dragged along whenever my mum and Mrs Pearce wanted to have tea and chat in our kitchen for

113

hours and hours and hours. I always got stuck having to 'entertain' her. Sometimes we pretended I was a famous movie star and Chloe was my biggest fan. I made her follow me around begging for my autograph while I ignored her or ran from her like she was the paparazzi. No matter how mean I was to her, she only seemed to worship me more.

"Well, I'll be off, then. Have fun, you two."

I was expecting Chloe to be overjoyed to see me. Normally she would have raced down the stairs shouting my name if she knew I was in the house. But this time she didn't appear until her mother had gone. I closed the front door and turned to see her on the landing, clutching a stuffed pony. It was blue and missing an eye and for some reason it made me feel sad for her.

"Hi Chloe."

She mumbled hello and came slowly down the stairs, where she stood staring up at me, her big eyes like melting chocolate.

I sighed. "Well, looks like I'm stuck here with you."

"For the whole night?"

"No, just a couple of hours. Didn't your mum tell you?"

"She's going on a *date*." She made it sound so important I had to laugh. No doubt her mother had told her it was her big chance to land another man. I'd overheard some of the desperate conversations she had with my mum.

"Yeah," I said. "A big date."

Chloe nodded solemnly. "So she won't be back tonight."

"What are you talking about? It's only seven now and you'll be asleep by the time she gets back."

"Last time she didn't come home," Chloe said. "Or the time before."

I stared at her while this sunk in. Mrs Pearce had lied to me! On the one hand it was rotten because you shouldn't lie to people – especially kids – but on the other hand, now I *definitely* wouldn't have to babysit for her ever again. My parents would be furious at her for lying to me.

Chloe was looking worried. "Emma? You won't leave me

all by myself, will you?"

"No, of course not. Don't be stupid."

She stared at me, her eyes wide and searching. "You promise? *Really* promise?"

Her intensity made me uneasy and I smiled to reassure her. "I promise."

Chloe heaved a huge sigh of relief and squeezed my hand and I found myself actually feeling sorry for her. The poor kid was probably so used to her mum tricking her that she didn't trust anyone – not even me. So I promised again.

"Does your mum do that a lot?" I asked. "Leave you by yourself?"

Chloe pursed her lips and looked away, twisting her body from side to side. The legs of the stuffed pony in her arms swung like they were broken, reminding me of the time I found my cat Ivan dead in the garden. I'd carried his limp body around for hours, feeling like he'd abandoned me.

"Sometimes," Chloe mumbled. "I don't like it here by myself. It's scary."

I felt a sudden surge of big-sisterly protectiveness towards her and I imagined ringing the police. I could just see the Armed Response Unit surrounding a posh restaurant on the TV, all spotlights and slow motion while a helicopter went chop-chop-chop overhead. As they dragged Mrs Pearce out and forced her into a police car, she saw me in the crowd and cried in her deep slowed-down voice that she was sorry, so very, very sorry. I stood shielding Chloe in my arms, unmoved by her pleas.

"Well, there's nothing to be afraid of," I said, but I was trying to convince myself too. I didn't like the idea of being alone in the house all night any more than Chloe did. I still slept with a night-light on in my bedroom. Not that I'd ever want anyone to know that.

Chloe glanced nervously at the darkened front windows, at the night that pressed against the glass like a giant pair of hands. She climbed up on a chair to reach the switch to turn on the porch light. A warm glow shone through the windows and she gave me a shy smile as she clambered back down.

I wasn't about to tell her off for wasting electricity; I was tempted to go through the house switching *all* the lights on.

"Are you afraid of them too?" Chloe asked as though reading my mind.

"Afraid of who?"

"The things that aren't there."

I didn't like the way she said it. The weight she gave to the words made me feel like we were being watched. "What things?"

She peered up the darkened staircase and my gaze followed hers. There was a patch of deep shadow where the stairs branched off from the landing. Anything could be lurking there unseen. I thought of the time I had reached inside a cupboard only to have a spider scuttle up my bare arm. I felt its tiny legs for weeks afterwards. With a shudder I turned back to Chloe. "There's nothing there. Stop trying to freak me out."

"I'm not," she said, looking fearful herself. "My mum says they're not there but they are. She just can't see them."

"See what?"

Chloe frowned as she tried to find the right words. "At first you can only see them when you're not looking. Like if you have to go to the loo at night and it's dark. They're right behind you but if you turn around to look, they slide back into the shadows. They live in the places where you've just been."

As she spoke I saw myself tiptoeing down a long dark hallway, sensing something behind me and whirling to confront it, only for it to vanish. I didn't want her to know how much she was scaring me. I particularly disliked her use of the word *slide*. It was too vivid, too specific.

"How do you know you aren't just imagining things?"

She looked wounded. "I'm not!" she cried. "They're real!"

"Okay, so what happens if you do see them? If you look right at them?"

Chloe squeezed her pony tighter and turned to face the

stairs. "I'm looking at one right now."

I felt my skin crawl as I stared into the shadows. "I can't see anything," I whispered, still straining to see. I yearned for the courage to stalk boldly up the stairs and prove there was nothing there. "Where is it?"

"It's halfway down."

Now I knew she was just trying to scare me. The first flight of steps was well lit and there was clearly nothing there. Determined to show her it was all in her head, I marched over to the stairs.

"Emma, don't—"

Chloe reached for me but I shook her off. I went up three steps and sure enough, the staircase was empty. The patch of shadows on the landing was empty too. Even so, I didn't want to go any further up. I turned back to her and spread my arms. "See?"

But Chloe was crouching on the floor, clinging to her stuffed toy and staring in wide-eyed terror. "It's *right there*," she hissed, pointing just to my left.

The space beside me was definitely empty. I waved my arm around where the thing was supposed to be and shook my head. "Nothing at all."

"You can't see them," she whispered fearfully, "but I can."

She was starting to scare me again. I glanced behind me and for a second I thought I'd seen something dart back into the shadows. Something long and thin. Something that would *slide*. I turned back to Chloe but I could sense it was still there. My heart started to beat faster and I told myself it was just my imagination. It was what my parents always said when I was scared. There was no long-armed man under the bed, no staring eye in my closet. Just my imagination. And Chloe's.

"Look," I said, heading back down the stairs, "no more monsters, okay? Let's watch a movie."

But as I reached the floor and turned towards the lounge I caught a flicker of movement out of the corner of my eye. A long slinky shape paced along behind me, like a shadow that was somehow heavy and real. Like something I would *feel* if it reached out to touch me. I stopped and spun around to see it, but it was too fast.

Chloe saw me and clutched at my hand. "You *do* see them!" she cried, sounding relieved and dismayed at the same time.

I wasn't comforted by the sudden thought that they were making themselves visible now that I knew they were there. From the stairs came a creak, like the sound a wolf might make sneaking up on its prey.

"You believe me now, don't you, Emma?"

I didn't want to admit it. What if admitting it made them even more real? I stared hard into the shadows beneath the hall table, the shadows along the wall, the shadows that swarmed like ants in every empty room. And I listened, straining to hear over the banging of my heart in my ears.

"They're getting closer," Chloe whimpered, her eyes filling with tears.

"Stop it! There's nothing there. You're just making it all up." I felt weird and a little sick as I said it and a strange thought came to me. Did grown-ups say things like that because there really *was* something there in the dark? Were they just as afraid? Mrs Pearce had lied to me. What if my parents had lied too? Did believing in lies make them real?

Chloe was clinging to me, soaking the leg of my jeans with tears as she begged and pleaded with me to make them go away. It wasn't fair. I was just a kid too.

I grabbed Chloe by the arms and shook her. "Look," I said, "they're not there. They're all in your head. Trust me. They're in your head and they can't get out."

And again I had that weird feeling. Like something was getting stronger with everything I said. Then I heard the laughter. So soft it might only have been in my mind. It sounded pleased, as though I'd done exactly what someone – or something – had wanted.

Chloe wasn't crying any more, but the look on her face was worse than tears. She looked empty. Her eyes were dark, like shadows. She stared at me, not seeing me. Not seeing anything. I let go of her and she slumped to the floor in a heap.

I shook her and called her name. "Chloe? Stop it; it isn't funny! Chloe, wake up!"

But she didn't respond. She didn't even blink as I waved my hands in front of her eyes. I crumpled to the floor as I realised what I'd done, what I'd said. *They're in your head and they can't get out.* She had believed me. Behind those blank eyes she was screaming but there was no way I could reach her. I cried and called to her for a while but I knew it was no use. She was gone.

Chloe had dropped her pony on the floor. I picked it up and held it but it only made me feel worse. I crept under the hall table where I couldn't see her vacant, staring eyes. The shadows wrapped themselves around me like arms but I knew they wouldn't hurt me. They'd got what they came for.

No one would believe me if I told them what really happened. But Mrs Pearce had lied to me, so I would lie to her too. What else could I do? I'd told her I wasn't good with kids.

119

BIT ON THE SIDE

Tom Johnstone

At first he didn't realise what the smell was.

Fortunately for him, neither did Clare.

"Any idea what that is, Nick? Smells like something just crawled in here and died."

"Must be one of the mice."

"Oh, I wish you'd just pull your finger out and deal with them – set a trap or something."

"A trap? What if Maisie finds it?"

"Alright! Alright! Hopefully it *is* one of the mice, but whatever it is, we can't leave it there. Maybe it's behind the fridge."

But they pulled the fridge out, and then the freezer: nothing.

"Maybe it's under the stairs then, I've spotted one scuttling into the cupboard there a couple of times", said Nick. "I'll go and have a look."

But when he left the kitchen, Clare couldn't smell it any more. Nick could though. It seemed to follow him around.

Clare had to leave for work, but drew back as he went to kiss her goodbye.

"Ugh! There it is again. Has it got onto you somehow?" she grimaced. "Look, please just try and sort it out before I get back, okay? Love you!"

While Maisie was playing in the front room, he had a clear-out of the below stairs cupboard. He found old papers from his student days, including his dissertation on Celtic religious practices; dust and cobwebs; an assortment of gadgets he had long been meaning to fix and the tools he had been meaning to fix them with; a peppering of mouse droppings; and a hole gnawed in the skirting board.

But no dead mouse.

And the smell remained. A sort of musty, musky, animal odour, alien yet strangely familiar.

He opened the back door to let some air into the kitchen, but it seemed as powerful as ever. He went upstairs, partly to escape the smell, partly to use the toilet. It was then that he noticed that it seemed to follow him. Perhaps he had brought it in himself, from the bottom of the garden, where the overgrown trees and shrubs encouraged stray cats and errant dogs to congregate and leave their pungent messages.

Downstairs Maisie was still happily chattering to herself, so he stripped off and jumped into the shower, scrubbing himself more vigorously than usual. He hadn't been that desperate to rid his body of a smell, since – since – Why *had* it been again? He felt better after the shower, but even as he towelled himself dry, he could feel himself breathing through his mouth. As he padded downstairs, he could no longer restrain his nostrils from twitching and letting in the odour that seemed to pervade everything.

Then he realised that Maisie was no longer in the front room.

He had forgotten that the back door was still open. The air still smelt rank and putrid. Not only had the door not let the fresh air in, it had let Maisie out.

And she wasn't in the garden – at least not where he could see her.

"Maisie!" he called, running towards the end of the garden. Nick knew that it led to a shambles of a back alley that joined all the houses on the street. Rubbish-strewn and overgrown though it was, an adventurous child could still find her way out to the road.

Not that Maisie was particularly adventurous, Nick remembered desperately: she'd never shown the slightest inclination to explore the back alley!

"Maisie!" he called.

And in the dead silence, he thought he could hear something that could be whispering or the rustle of dry leaves, then Maisie's answering prattle. He blundered into the straggly, dark euonymus, clinging spider webs tickling his face. He heard a sound that could have been leaves again, only this time wet.

"Maisie?" His voice was softer now, but it trembled.

"Daddy!" she called from behind a rusty bin, as though jumping out from a game of hide-and-seek. The putrefying reek seemed very strong here. It didn't surprise him. All the neighbourhood dogs did their business here.

But this was a different smell.

"Come away from here, Maisie," he said. "Come on, let's go inside, and take your shoes off before you do."

They sat on the couch together, and watched Cbeebies together for a while, but Maisie didn't snuggle up to him as usual. She said he "smelled funny."

"It must be the lady," she said, almost casually, still gazing at *The Night Garden*.

"What lady?" asked Nick.

"She smells like that, all muddy and nasty," said Maisie. "Have you met her too, daddy?"

On the TV, Igglepiggle and his friends prattled in their soothing nonsense language. Something was crawling like a spider through the back of Nick's mind.

"No," he said. "Is that what you were doing at the bottom of the garden?"

"She want to show me her baby," said Maisie. "She said it's my baby sister."

Nick got up and switched off the TV, silencing the cooing hum of the programme, but drawing wails of protest from Maisie. Outside dusk was beginning to spread its pall over the garden. After he had calmed her down, he said:

"Maisie, you know it's not very nice to play tricks on daddy."

"Yes," she said softly, her voice slightly husky from bawling, her face all sticky with tears and snot made thicker by her cold.

"And you know you shouldn't say things that aren't true."

"But it *is* true, daddy! She said to come back after this day, then she show me the baby!"

She was crying again, so he held her and gently stroked her soft curls.

Eventually she calmed down, and asked: "Can I have Night Garden on again?"

"Alright then," he sighed.

He didn't really think Maisie was making it up, even though it was what he wanted to believe. The more he thought about it, the closer and tighter he held her, as they listened to the narrator's soporific murmur. Usually, it was enough to send him into a light doze, but not this time. That invisible spider was still spinning a web whose gossamer threads were tickling awake parts of his brain he preferred to keep dormant. As the Cbeebies moving nursery wallpaper faded away, Nick could hear the slowing and deepening of Maisie's breathing, and feel her heaviness against him. So he carefully lifted her, and carried her upstairs to bed.

Maisie's breathing sounded a little wheezy, so he wanted to open her window, just to let the night air in. But he checked himself. The window looked out into the garden. He thought about what Maisie had told him about the bottom of the garden, and the window remained shut. About twenty minutes later, from the landing, he could hear the mucus building up in his daughter's nose and throat. It sounded worryingly like croup. He decided to open the window a chink and stay in her bedroom. Outside he could hear the leaves rustling on the path, they seemed to be whispering:

Remember the rule of three.

*

"Nick, what are you doing down there?"

He jerked awake on the floor. Clare was standing there. He couldn't quite read her expression in the dim illumination of the night-light. He felt cold and stiff from the chill night air coming in through the open window.

"Maisie was wheezing quite a bit, so I wanted to stay with her."

"Oh, Nick," said Clare. Her gentleness made him feel ashamed. "Come to bed," she said, holding a hand out to help him up.

Luckily, Maisie's breathing sounded a lot easier, because he didn't want to leave the room without locking her bedroom window.

"What time is it?" he asked Clare.

"One thirty."

"Tough night?" he asked as they lay in bed.

"Delivered a dead one," she said, her voice low and flat. "That shook me up a bit. Worse for the mother of course. I always thought if I was going to miscarry, I'd want it to happen in the first trimester, not like this with the baby almost to term. Imagine going through all that just to give birth to a corpse."

She sighed.

"Look, if you're just going to fall asleep, don't bother asking. I don't particularly want to go through the whole thing again just for my own benefit. Jesus! There's that awful smell again. Nick, it's not you, is it? When did you last shower?"

"I had one this afternoon," he protested, "and I wasn't asleep, I was just thinking."

He was thinking: 'trimester', the division of pregnancy into three phases, three times three months.

He was thinking, you've delivered a dead baby from a live mother –

But have you ever delivered a live baby from a dead one?

He was thinking about Verity.

*

After her exhausting shift, Clare soon drifted off.

But Nick didn't find it so easy. He lay there listening out for Maisie's congested breathing next door, and also thinking about the things she had said. She was an imaginative child, but how could she have known about Verity?

When Clare had started working longer and longer shifts at the birth centre, Nick had opted to stay at home and look after Maisie, occasionally taking in clients for his small but expanding massage business. That was how he had met Verity. Clare had become very absorbed in her profession, and despite (or perhaps because of) her commitment to the principles of independent midwifery, she had a certain impatience for what she saw as his preciousness about homeopathy and alternative medicine.

Verity on the other hand had shared his New Age ideals, and described herself as both 'single' and 'a wiccan' in her Facebook profile, as well as 'interested in men'. She was lonely, attractive and seemed appealingly vulnerable, with those wide, dark brown eyes. Nick's solitary house-husbandry had left him open to temptation from her lithe and slender limbs. It may come as no surprise that their weekly massage had turned into something more. That was why he had showered so vigorously in those heady days – to rid himself of Verity's powerful scent before Clare got home.

But her pregnancy had come as a surprise to Nick – or rather a shock that had caused him to lose his temper, when she had come to confront him with the news one morning. He was usually a very calm person, but her behaviour had amounted to unusual provocation. Anyone would have understood his reaction. Well, maybe not Clare, with her Women's Studies degree and her Radical Midwives' group.

Clare was at work, and Maisie was at nursery. It seemed to Nick that Verity was exploiting her knowledge of the family's routine. Perhaps it was anger at this that had made Nick react so violently – although it had never bothered him before, when Verity had visited him on other weekday mornings when Maisie was at nursery.

But there was another reason for his uncharacteristic fit of rage. He had known that there was a risk of conception,

125

because both of them had rejected contraception, whether pill or prophylactic, in favour of more natural methods – using Verity's knowledge of her own menstrual cycle to minimise that risk. But as she had stood before him, half way up the staircase that led down to a flagged stone floor, her wild eyes challenging him as she held her hands under her fertile belly, like Clare's statue of *Sheila Na Gig*, he had wondered if she had deceived him about this.

He had been retreating upwards dodging as she grabbed at his hands, tears forming in her eyes as she tried to rekindle their extinguished affair, then anger as she threatened to return at a time when both Clare and Maisie were around. The exchange had grown more heated. He remembered thinking about what he'd read about *Sheila Na Gig* at college, the monstrous goddess with her *vagina dentata*, the devouring mother who at that moment seemed about to consume his life. His memory of what happened afterwards was at best hazy. He'd snapped under extreme provocation, and after that? Well, Verity hadn't bothered him much since then.

Until now.

*

A few minutes after he had finally fallen asleep, the noise woke Nick up. Clare was too deeply asleep to wake up. It was a hiccoughing cry from Maisie's room. Perhaps her wheezing had woken her up. Nick pulled his purple tie-dyed leggings on over his skinny legs, tied his long, straggly hair up in a tight bun, and went in. She was sat bolt upright in bed, staring into space, keening like a wounded seal cub.

Nick took her by the shoulders, not knowing what to do. She was staring right through him, as though he wasn't there, her cries turning into screams. He wanted to wake her up, but how could she be asleep with her eyes wide open?

He turned to the bedroom window.

Cautiously he opened it. The first thing he noticed was that an owl was hooting. But that wasn't all.

There was someone outside. Her scent had been so powerful in life – it was stronger than ever now.

He flung it open, and saw her. Mud streaked what was left of Verity's face, and leaf mould from the woods where he'd laid her to rest, or tried to. While one emaciated arm rocked a shapeless, grey bundle, the other held up the fingers left on the other hand, all three of them. The dark brown eyes were still there, open, large and unblinking, burning in the darkness.

Now he remembered what had happened when she had "happened to be passing" and just thought she'd "pop round" that day, the time she'd threatened to tell all.

After he had lashed out at her in anger, he remembered wanting to apologise, and tell her he wasn't the sort of man who did those things, that the man who had done them was not him.

But he couldn't.

Because she wasn't listening.

She was lying still on the stone floor at the bottom of the staircase.

She wasn't quite dead yet, she was gurgling, gargling blood, but words were forcing themselves out through the red bubbles, surprisingly clear considering her fractured jaw.

And here she was again, harassing him at night, that same jaw, flapping away like a shed door with a hinge missing in a gale, trying to form words. At first, no sound came out, just a sort of wet rasping, like the sound she had made at the bottom of the stairs. She was crooning to the rhythm of her rocking, a grating lullaby.

He screwed his eyes shut: *this isn't happening.*

When he opened his eyes, Verity was no longer there. Maybe she had shuffled away with her pathetic burden. It was only then that Nick noticed: Maisie had flopped back down to sleep, a few fitful sniffles the only evidence of any disturbance.

But he realised the child had finally calmed down when Verity's broken mouth had started forcing out its rough music, the lullaby that included the ones that had frothed from those ragged lips on the flagstone at the bottom of the stairs:

"Don't forget the rule of three!"

It was Verity, not he, that had soothed the child's night terrors and sung her to sleep.

*

The following morning, after struggling to get Maisie to nursery, in the face of both his and his child's tiredness from their disturbed night, he hit upon the idea.

He remembered going through the under-stair cupboard the day before, glancing at his dissertation, its pages all brown and grainy with dust. While researching it, he had read extensively about some of the things the ancient Celts had done when burying their dead, particularly their womenfolk. In his paper, he had noticed a passage about the inhumation of the corpses of witches and village 'scolds', where Celtic tribesmen took special measures to make sure the bodies stayed dead. There was one particular case in Dorset, where an extra mutilation had occurred to prevent the woman in question from talking, as well as walking.

At first he dismissed the idea from his mind. He didn't really believe all this, did he? But after what he had seen last night – or thought he'd seen – he wasn't so sure.

And what about the 'rule of three'? The figure last night had held up three fingers. Verity had mentioned this when talking to Nick about her pagan beliefs.

"Don't ever cross me, Nick," she had said, pulling at his lapels.

"Why not?"

"Because we wiccans believe that everything you do comes back on you threefold."

He had smiled uneasily.

"Sort of like karma?" he asked.

She had nodded, a half-smile playing on her pale lips.

Like many of his age and background, Nick subscribed to a vague notion of 'karma', but it wasn't a literal belief. Had Verity really believed all this? Come to that, did *he* now believe she'd come to his daughter's window and sung her to sleep? Maybe he'd fallen asleep in Maisie's room, and dreamed the whole thing. It certainly seemed less real in daylight.

Nevertheless, he didn't want to hear any more words or songs real or imagined from those pale lips, or what remained of them. And in his half-baked but dogged and obsessive way, he certainly believed in the power of ritual to 'sort things out'.

So he drove out to the woods in the mid-autumn rain with a spade and a saw, dug through a thick layer of earth and leaf mould until he found flesh, and fighting the urge to retch at the stench, carefully sawed the head from the body and then severed the jaw from the head (the last bit wasn't too hard – the jaw was broken after all). These he then placed at Verity's feet, taking care to point the head down towards the underworld, before replacing the pile of dirt and stamping it down. He worked efficiently, so that he still had over three quarters of an hour to shower and change his clothes before picking up Maisie from nursery. With something like satisfaction, he noticed that he could no longer smell Verity in the house.

His sense of relief had left him so relaxed that he was a little late collecting Maisie. Well, more than a little late, he realised as he saw the last few parents trailing out of the nursery school gates. And the staff cleaning up bright splashes of spilled paint and putting colourful toys away into drawers.

Maisie was sitting quietly on the mat where the children waited to be collected. She was on her own, the last one. She had her back to Nick, so he couldn't see her face.

Rather than sending Maisie out to Nick, as was the usual practice, the nursery teacher beckoned him inside the classroom.

"Maisie wanted to show you the picture she drew today," the

teacher said to him, then calling over to the solitary child on the carpet, "didn't you, Maisie?"

Maisie didn't answer, or turn round.

"Well, anyway, here it is." Nick noticed that the teacher was giving him an odd look, making her cheekbones stand out harshly in the declining light of the day, as she fussed around the various sheets of paper on the table. "And her artistic abilities are certainly going from strength to strength," she added, then lowering her voice and frowning a little, "although I was a little disturbed by the picture ..."

Get on with it, thought Nick irritably.

Finally, she produced the work of art.

Though drawn with a four-year-old's crudeness, it clearly depicted a pretty, smiling, little girl with blonde curly hair, holding hands with a woman, whose free arm cradled a smudged, grey shape. The woman and the girl were standing in front of a row of trees, which seemed to represent a forest, complete with an owl in one of the branches. The owl reminded Nick of Winnie the Pooh. The rest of the picture didn't. The ground, which Maisie had drawn in brown felt-tip, was flat, apart from what looked like a shallow hole next to the woman. Almost as if to make up for the missing piece of ground, there were brown splodges all over the woman's body.

"'Me with Verity and my baby sister'", Nick read. "Did you write that?" he asked.

"I wrote what Maisie asked me to write," replied the teacher, her voice hardening at the note of accusation in his.

"Well, she does have a very vivid imagination," said Nick, trying to force a note of levity into his voice. Seeing no softening in the teacher's expression he adopted a more sombre tone: "I suppose she's seen the missing person posters around the town."

"Yes," the teacher agreed, "it's certainly a very good likeness of Verity Keith – well, apart from ..."

The ghastly, skeletal body? The bright-red felt-tip gash on the head?

130

"But where *does* she get these ideas?" wondered the teacher.

"I've no idea," shrugged Nick. "Why don't we ask *her*?"

And they both turned towards where Maisie was sitting.

To where Maisie *had* been sitting.

"Who left that open?" said the teacher, striding towards a fire door that led out into a neglected and overgrown part of the school grounds, where ivy had eaten into the brickwork of the perimeter wall, causing parts of it to crumble to the ground.

It was then that the burden of Verity's croaked out lullaby popped back into his head:

Come, little one, and walk with me,
  Don't forget the rule of three.

Soon Nick could hear the teacher outside, calling his daughter's name. He had been about to follow her example, but now he noticed the smell like something rotten in his throat. It was coming from near the fire door, from the sideboard where the staff left paintbrushes and pots to dry after being washed. He could hear a slow dripping into the sink, and saw that what was dripping was black and sticky.

Come, little one, and you shall see,
  You and she and me makes three.

The smell was sticking to his lungs like rank treacle. And he saw that something stealthy and silent had left him an offering, like a cat that brings you the gift of a half-eaten bird or rodent. The difference was that Verity had left something of herself there: three things. The jaw lay a few inches away from the rest of the head, and Nick saw and heard that the third part of the gift wriggled and mewled in its damp, grey sacking.

INDECENT BEHAVIOUR

Marion Pitman

It was Thursday night; Jason's pay had run out and Lenny's giro was late, so they left the pub early. Outside the bar the cool air smelled of smoke, the pavement was covered with fag ends.

"What shall we do then?" said Lenny

"Not much *to* do," said Jason.

"Let's go down the late night Paki and nick some booze."

"They don't open after nine, not since the last time."

"I know – let's go down the Feathers and duff up a queer."

Jason made a face; "It's a long walk."

"Well, what then?"

"Oh all right. Might as well I suppose. There's always cops round the Feathers." Jason was a pessimist.

Lenny, who hadn't the brains to be a pessimist, laughed. "The filth won't take no notice. They're after the poofters. We'll be doing 'em a favour."

"Probably rain again."

*

They stood in a doorway across the road from the Prince of Wales Feathers, watching men come in and out in groups and couples; some wore uniform leather and chains and large moustaches, but most looked worryingly like Jason and Lenny, in T-shirts and denims or combats, some with jackets, some without, in that uncertain season between spring and summer.

Jason started to get nervous, folded a stick of gum into his mouth, and said, "Come on, this is a waste of time."

"No, hang on, there's one now. That old geezer."

"Uh. Okay."

The man who came out on his own and walked briskly away from the town centre was smallish, in his sixties, with neat

132

silver hair, very dapper in a light suit, pink shirt and cravat. He walked with small, quick steps; on the far side of the road they kept pace with him easily.

Once out of sight of the pub they crossed the road, and he became aware of them. He walked faster, not quite running. The streets were deserted, lined with closed and often empty shops, small workshops, offices; half the streetlamps were out. The side turnings were darker than the main road. Soon they came alongside a breaker's yard, opposite a parade of lockup shops, half of them boarded up, all of them shut. A rat scuttled out of the yard and disappeared in the darkness.

They walked faster; Jason moved out to one side. The old man stopped under a solitary streetlamp. Lenny grinned with all his teeth, like a shark, and said, "Hallo, Grandad."

*

Two weeks later, Lenny had a nasty turn in the Gents at the pub, when the navvy at the next urinal put a hand on his prick. At least, Lenny thought, it must have been him; there was no one else in there. Lenny was rather small and skinny; the navvy was six-four and built like a brick shithouse, and the look Lenny got when he said, "Oy—" shut him up; but what kept him quiet afterwards was the fact that the navvy had hands like legs of pork, sunburnt and hairy, whereas the hand Lenny had felt and seen on his privates was small, soft, white and well-manicured.

He went back into the bar, a little bit shaky. After about half an hour Jason came in, looking worried, holding an evening paper. He pulled Lenny over to a corner and spoke in a hoarse whisper: "'Ere, Len. You know that old queer we done over? He died."

"Couldn't of."

"Well he bloody did."

"Must've put the boot in too hard."

Jason threw down the paper, and went to the bar for a couple of pints. When he came back, Lenny said, "D'you reckon the filth'll be after us?"

Jason drank about half his pint and thought about it; in the end pessimism lost out to practicality – "Nah," he said, "who seen us?"

"Yeah, right." Lenny grinned, cheerful again. He forgot about the nasty moment in the Gents.

*

Next day, Jason got home from work feeling horny. As he banged the flat door, waking the baby, Sharon put his tea on the table, and was surprised to hear him say, "Never mind the tea, get 'em off."

"What?"

"You heard, get your pants off."

Bugger, she thought, now he'll complain the tea's cold. She took off her skirt, tights and knickers; he was more impatient than usual, shoving her hard on the couch and flinging himself on top of her – and all at once the prick pushing at her thigh went soft as a whelk. He grunted and jerked back, staring in disbelief. She reached for him, but he pushed her hand away and got up, angrily pulling up his pants and zipping his fly. As he made for the door she – stupidly, she realised – said, "Jas? What about your tea?" at which he picked up the plate and flung it hard at the wall. The baby began to cry; Jason slammed the front door. Sharon took a deep breath, put on her skirt, and picked up the sausage and broken china and most of the chips; she put them in the kitchen bin, then got a cloth and dabbed half-heartedly at the baked beans oozing down the wall.

*

Jason headed for the pub, pushing out of his mind the fact that what had seemed to put him off at the last minute was Sharon's body – the fact that it was female.

It was early; the bar was almost empty. He ordered a pint. The barman was new – clean-shaven, neatly dressed and good-looking. Poofter, thought Jason. He drank half the beer, and sat moodily watching the barman serving in the saloon. He only looked about nineteen, tall, slim, with a small, neat arse. Jason started to feel randy again. He made himself think about Sharon, although he was watching the barman's bum. He thought about Sharon's bum. He finished his beer, and went back home.

She was sitting on the bed reading a magazine, still naked under her skirt. He threw the magazine aside, pulling up her skirt as he unzipped. He shut his eyes as he thrust, and this time almost made it, but not quite; her femaleness was too insistent. She began to sympathise, which was the last straw; he smacked her across the face, and stumbled out, pulling up his trousers; he went to the off-licence for a bottle of Scotch, took it home, and drank himself insensible in the living room.

*

Two days after that, on the bus to work, Jason suddenly caught his breath, and jerked his thighs together. It felt as if – something – were in his underpants. He looked down, not knowing what he expected to see, but all he saw was the crotch of his trousers slightly stirred by the beginnings of arousal. He felt a hand – a small, smooth hand – stroking his balls, fondling his prick, expertly turning him on. The pleasure, though, was utterly drowned in embarrassment, bewilderment and horror. He had to stand and walk very awkwardly getting off the bus, and breathed a huge sigh of relief as the hand ceased its attentions as he entered the workshop, and his excitement diminished before any of his workmates could notice. He tried to put the experience out of his mind, telling himself he'd been drinking too much, that his failure to get it up with Sharon was affecting his mind. Perhaps he should find a tart – but to be embarrassed like that with a tart would be worse, and cost money as well. It was just one of those things. He wouldn't think about it.

But the hand came back, next day, and the days after, at work, on the bus. Jason began to acquire a permanently hunched posture, and inevitably had to endure crude cracks from the blokes at work. He stayed away from the pub for a few days, but he found it wasn't only the barman: everywhere he was conscious of young men in tight jeans, the slight bulge at the crotch, the way their buttocks moved against each other. The hard-on seldom lasted till he got back to Sharon; once when it did, he told her to take off her skirt and tights and put her jeans on. She stared at him.

"Are you stupid?" he shouted, "I want to fuck you in your jeans. Is that too hard to understand? Can you hear me?"

She went on staring, but backed away and went into the bedroom; he followed her; as she got the jeans halfway up, he pushed her face first against the wall with one hand, freeing himself with the other, and entered her from behind, his eyes closed, in his mind thrusting between the cheeks of a plump, pretty boy. He came, cataclysmically, and immediately went to the bathroom and was sick.

He didn't try again. He masturbated a lot, and took out his feeling of helplessness in smacking Sharon and shaking the baby when it cried.

One morning when he was too hungover to protest, Sharon said, why didn't he go to the doctor?

"Yeah," he said, "that's likely." What would he say? 'Doctor, I can't get it up with a woman'? 'Doctor I'm suddenly turning queer'? Yeah, right.

He tried to keep telling himself it was Sharon that was the problem, and wondered if he should try and pick up one of the slags they met down the pub, but he knew he wouldn't. The humiliation would be public then.

After another couple of weeks, Jason came home and found the flat empty. He cursed, wondering who Sharon was out

gossiping with. Her bloody sister or her mum, or that bitch
Kayley. There was no food in the kitchen; he cursed again and
went out for a kebab. It wasn't till he was eating it in front of
the TV that he noticed an emptiness on the shelf unit next to
the set, where Sharon's Mills and Boons and fat chick-lit
paperbacks lived. He puzzled about it till he finished his meal,
then went into the bedroom. A lot of clothes were gone from
the wardrobe; the baby's things were gone; in the bathroom the
shelves were practically empty.

When he realised she wasn't coming back, it was almost a
relief. He made no attempt to find her. He lived on takeaways,
and slept a lot.

*

There was a new apprentice at work, just sixteen, with soft
yellow hair and a pink and white prettiness. Jason couldn't
help seeing him, all the time. The desire grew, and the hand
got to work, stroking and fondling. He went to the toilet, and
tried to masturbate himself to orgasm, but his excitement
abated as soon as he was on his own. He went back, and the
hand began again; just before lunchtime it brought him to a
climax.

He felt himself blushing scarlet; he heard men sniggering,
and when he looked up he found the supervisor giving him a
filthy look. When the lunch break came he muttered to the
supervisor that he had food poisoning, and went without
waiting for an answer.

He went to the library and found Lenny, reading the papers.
He'd finished the Sun and started on the Mirror.

Jason said, "Come down the pub."

"What, now?" said Lenny, in a library whisper.

"They're open all day, aren't they? Come on."

It was three pints and a whisky chaser before he could start
to talk about it. "Len," he said, "what'd you say if I told you I
was – I was – haunted?"

137

Lenny started and slopped his beer. "Haunted? What d'you mean? What by?"

"Well … by – by a hand, I suppose."

"Oh god. Oh god. It's got you too, then."

Hesitantly, they told each other the things the hand had done, the terrible appetites it had aroused. After a couple more drinks, Jason went to the Gents. Lenny followed him in.

When they had finished, and turned to come out, they looked at each other. The toilet was empty. Without a word, they went into a cubicle, and bolted the door; gently, lovingly, unwillingly, in the cramped and stinking stall, they touched each other, kissed, undressed, handled and sucked and pleasured each other …

Afterwards, white-faced, silent, they walked out of the pub in opposite directions.

*

Jason went back to his empty flat and hanged himself in his belt. Sharon found him a week later when she went back for the rest of her shoes.

Lenny, who was too stupid to be a pessimist, went home to his mum, and knocked her down out of habit, and locked himself in his bedroom. Over the next few days his behaviour was so bizarre that when his mum called the police, after he threw a saucepan of boiling cabbage at her and knocked himself unconscious trying to fling himself out of a closed window, she persuaded them to section him. She put it all down to drugs.

In the hospital he lay still, masturbating constantly, and never speaking except when he looked up, smiled sweetly, and said, "Hallo, Grandad."

HIS FAMILY

Kate Farrell

You know the moment when a police officer settles the prisoner in the car? You must have seen it countless times in television dramas. Hand on the prisoner's head to protect it always. It's a simple enough task and yet sometimes one of the hardest parts of my job. On more than one occasion I have wanted to smash the prisoner's skull against the doorframe, when I have just witnessed his, or sometimes even her, handiwork. Reminds me of the old police brutality joke. Question: How did the copper crack open his egg? Answer: He didn't, sarge, it slipped on its way down to the cell. What would push an upstanding professional officer, highly trained to deal with any eventuality, to seriously consider it?

Damien Roth was singularly unremarkable in appearance, a fact alone that could have made him special. His lightly pocked skin had the slightly oily texture of damp putty; his hair, to describe it as sandy over dignified it, his eyelashes were practically nonexistent, the colour of his eyes somewhere between dun and khaki; he was small, almost dainty, yet wiry and strong. There was something of the jockey about him. Very self-contained, strangely he had no presence, no aura, and his mushroom coloured hospital uniform did little to dispel the sensation. He was easy to overlook.

He said it was simple enough to gain employment at the hospital two years ago. Checks were less stringent then and there was always a demand for porters, those unsung and unheralded operatives who ferry around the sick, the dying and the dead, or even just some of their component parts. Wheelchairs and stretchers for the whole or nearly whole; buckets for the discarded limbs. All in a day's work. Very nasty, but someone's got to do it.

Damien enjoyed patrolling the hospital grounds and

corridors even when not on duty. Had he been questioned about this, he would have responded that it was important to find the fastest and easiest routes round the hospital's sprawl for his charges, such was his diligence. He was unremarkable and quiet, did not join the union to picket for better pay and conditions, yet would always contribute whenever asked for a donation to a colleague's gift. He appeared punctually for his shifts and never watched the clock when going home time was approaching. According to his superiors, all in all a model employee.

The hospital consisted of two buildings on the same site. The newer part, built at the end of the twentieth century, accommodated Accident and Emergency, wards and operating theatres; the older building, four storeys high and constructed in the middle of the preceding century, housed only the administration functions for personnel and finance, in a small suite of rooms confined to the ground floor. When bureaucracy and fundraising permitted, they too intended to move to another new extension. The first and second floors were used for storage, though who would want rusting bedsteads, trolleys and wheelchairs, bent food trays and chipped utility crockery? The top two floors were surplus to requirements, and nobody we spoke to among the hospital staff could ever recall the need to visit them. There had been a grandiose scheme to redevelop this older wing into luxury flats, but in the light of recent events such homes may prove undesirable.

Damien Roth's knowledge of the hospital layout naturally included the older part. Of particular interest was the top floor, served at the rear entrance by an elderly if functional lift, which was accessed by a concertina door. It grated and clattered but reached its destination for all that, like some decrepit old dowager wheezing her way upstairs to the attic.

The windows on the top floors hadn't been cleaned for literally decades. Light barely filtered through even on the brightest of days, while cracked linoleum on the floors rendered the surfaces unsafe in the half-light. Damien Roth, however, was as sure of his footing as he was of everything else. Over a period of time he had been gathering some basic items of furniture, a bed, chairs, a table, some filing cabinets. He found too a defunct television set, which he placed on top of a filing cabinet, as he gradually assembled his twilight home. Cups and plates, moth eaten blankets, old stained pillows. All the domestic paraphernalia needed was found two floors down, and transported aloft.

But there was something missing.

William Mason sat in the hospital reception area with his overnight bag on his lap, waiting for his daughter Dorothy, to come and collect him. She was rather late, but she had such a busy and full life, and she said she'd pick him up after she had dropped her husband off at the airport, away on another business trip. He was due to stay at Dorothy's only for a short period of convalescence after a nasty bout of emphysema, before returning to his own ground floor flat. This was near enough to his daughter for emergencies, but not too close so it interfered with her interesting and varied schedule.

William checked his wristwatch. She really was very late. No doubt the traffic was bad, and it was asking a lot of her to come and collect him. She'd be along soon enough, and then they'd get to her house and have a lovely cup of tea, and he would wait for his grandsons to come in from school and …

"Hallo, Mr Mason, you've been here a while, haven't you?"

It was that nice porter, the quiet fellow. Darren, or something.

"Darren, hello. I'm waiting for my daughter; she's coming to collect me. I expect she'll be along any time now …"

"Yes, I know, I've just seen her. She's having a spot of bother finding a place to park, so she's asked me to take you out to her."

"Thank you, Darren, thank you very much, if it's no trouble."

"No trouble at all, Mr Mason. You don't want to sit here all day, it's like a madhouse. Let's get you outside."

Damien released the brake on William's wheelchair, and steered him through the controlled bedlam of hospital reception. He pushed him around the side of the building, away from its clamour and security, towards the old wing. William was confused; his lungs and his legs were all but useless, but there was little wrong with his eyesight.

"Where are we going, Darren?"

"She said she'd wait around the back here, so you just sit back and enjoy the ride. We can take a short cut through the old building."

William Mason sat back and enjoyed the ride as he'd been instructed, thinking that the longed for cup of tea was getting nearer.

"If you don't mind me asking, Mr Mason, how old are you?"

"All the sixes, clickety click," replied his passenger, a lifelong fan of bingo. Dorothy and her husband preferred bridge and backgammon.

"Perfect," said Damien, "that's about the same age as my dad."

They entered the old wing by the back entrance, and in the far distance the sounds of office life trickled down the corridors. The lift was already on the ground floor, the door open like a yawning mouth at feeding time. Its mechanism could not be heard in the administration suites. Damien had checked. William, curious if not concerned, tried to turn round in the wheelchair and question Damien, but the porter just gave him an encouraging pat on the shoulder and shushed him, as if a child. They rode up in it to the top floor where the air hung heavy and musty, as if undisturbed for decades. Damien pushed him down a maze of corridors and eventually they arrived at a large open area with chairs and a television set. William was having some difficulty breathing in the stale atmosphere, which added to his growing sense of unease. Ignoring his questions, Damien lifted him out of the wheelchair, sat him in one of the upright armchairs, and leant

142

over him to adjust his scarf. A casual observer might have been touched by his seeming concern for the older man.

"Now then, we don't want you catching cold, do we, Mr Mason?"

He gave the scarf a sudden final adjustment, and William fought for breath, his hands flapping aimlessly like injured birds in the vicinity of his throat. His eyes pleaded with Damien's, but all he saw was dun pools, dead and inert. He tried to speak and the last word he would ever utter was a stranger's name:

"Darr-en ..."

His eyes bulged while his skin was turning the colour of the blue stripe in his scarf, his protruding tongue a shade somewhere between dove grey and magenta.

"It's Damien, Mr Mason. That is, *Damien*."

Eventually Damien Roth loosened the scarf, made sure that William was settled comfortably in his chair, and then made the return journey to the main hospital, and always the considerate employee, replaced the wheelchair in reception. On his way he passed William's daughter. A harassed receptionist, who was still waiting to be relieved for her lunch break at ten minutes to three, had told her that her father had made other arrangements for transport to his own home, owing to the lateness of her arrival. Dorothy was not best pleased with this information, typical of the old bugger, and she resolved to let him stew awhile and not phone him for a day or two.

Audrey Lomax was waiting for her hip replacement operation. Though relatively young, only sixty, she had been plagued for some years with a bad hip, exacerbated by osteoporosis. A major flu epidemic suddenly hit the hospital, staff members from all departments were absenting themselves, and extra cover was needed whenever and wherever possible. Damien, unaffected by the virus, was happy to work extra shifts. He was feeling lucky. Rosters and administration suffered during the flu spell, but Audrey Lomax's hip replacement operation was not affected. Her pre-med was administered, leaving her conscious but light-headed, and Damien was asked to wheel her stretcher to Theatre Number Two, where her surgeon, Mr Reynolds would be waiting. On her ward, a telephone rang unanswered for some while. Such luck that Damien happened to be passing and in the absence of any nursing staff, he took the call. He was informed that Mr Reynolds's list was to be cancelled, as he too that very morning had succumbed to the virus. Such luck indeed.

Damien wheeled Audrey Lomax from the sanctuary of the new wing to his eyrie in the old building. She was groggy, not fully awake, but when he steered the stretcher from the elevator towards her destination, the smell that greeted her made her gag. William Mason had been sitting in his chair for three days, and he had urinated as he died. Despite her semi-drugged state and the pervading penumbra, Audrey knew there was something very wrong. This wasn't the way to the operating theatre surely. What was this place of foul smelling shadows? She was attempting to breathe through her mouth because of the stench, which she could not easily identify, but she had to try and talk to the porter in whose care she lay. However, like a fly in the spider's web she wasn't so much in his care, as at his mercy. Her voice seemed to belong to somebody else, still she managed:

"What's this place? Where are we?"

Damien paused briefly, produced a small jar of Vick's from his pocket and smeared some under his nose. He ignored her question, the spasm of retching that it produced, and continued wheeling her towards a group of chairs. One of them seemed to be already occupied as far as Audrey could tell, though streaming eyes impaired her vision. The unnameable odour was becoming even stronger.

"Look who I found outside, Dad," he said. "Look who's been hiding from us. Now come on, Mum, let's get you settled and then we can have a nice cup of tea together."

He raised her to a sitting position, lifted her off the trolley and placed her in an upright chair, next to William Mason. He lifted one of William's hands, disregarded the cracking sound he heard as he manoeuvred the wrist, and placed the arid and scaly paw on Audrey's arm, as if in welcome.

"Ah. Look at that, Dad's really pleased to see you," said Damien.

Her sedation was insufficient to lessen the horror of the smell, the sight, and now the touch of the old man, and she tried to scream. A feeble bubbling sound emerged, for her throat had the consistency of sandpaper. She pressed back into the chair, a pathetic attempt to put some little distance between herself and William's mouldering cadaver.

"What's that, Mum, you feeling a bit chilly?" Damien did a comedy mock shiver. "You know, you're right, it is a bit parky in here. Lucky I've got just the thing to warm you up."

He untied the blue striped scarf from William's neck without disturbing the older man unduly, stood behind Audrey Lomax and tied it round her neck, until she could feel the cold no longer.

Yes, eventually of course the police were summoned. Two patients had seemingly vanished into thin air, no records of removal, no apparent sightings, a hospital in chaos and confusion, and yes, of course, my colleagues searched some of the buildings and the grounds, as it was a very serious matter, but no clues to the whereabouts of William Mason and Audrey Lomax were established. The police station had not escaped the flu epidemic, and we too were under resourced, so our searches were not as thorough as you might reasonably hope for.

Ian Marshall was one of the least badly injured victims of a major traffic accident, which occurred about a week after the police had provided no satisfactory reasons for the disappearance of two not very elderly patients. He sat in

145

Accident and Emergency, stunned and concussed, holding a temporary dressing to a head wound, while waiting for a doctor to check him over thoroughly.

Damien had been quietly ferrying patients from triage to other cubicles or x-ray, doing whatever was required of him. He noticed Ian Marshall sitting unattended and thought perhaps he could help. As he assisted him into a wheelchair, he said:

"Has anyone taken your details down yet?"

Ian shook his head, no. He'd given his name to somebody, a very young nurse a while ago, and that was all. Damien was sympathetic.

"That won't do at all, will it? We must get you seen to, mustn't we?"

Ian was really in quite a bad way, and leant back in the chair as Damien set off. Soon they reached the rear entrance to the old wing, but Ian's eyes were closed. He didn't know where he was, and he cared even less. The car he had been travelling in, the woman who had been beside him, the children fighting on the back seat, the jack-knifed lorry, the damp and greasy road surface; he was reliving the crash in storyboard format.

They seemed to be going up in a lift. The porter spoke to him:

"How old are you?"

He didn't answer – his scrambled thoughts were elsewhere.

The porter punched his shoulder. The question again.

"I said, how old are you?"

"Twenty-eight."

"That's nearly perfect," said Damien Roth. "I'm thirty-two."

When the elevator arrived at the fourth floor, Damien opened the concertina doors and pushed his newest charge towards the seating area where William and Audrey waited for them. Despite Ian's semi-comatose state, the odour that assailed his sinuses had the effect of smelling salts on his system. He jerked upright in his wheelchair, and blood flowed down his brow and into his eyes. The scene he beheld spectacularly surpassed the horror of the carnage in which he'd just participated.

It was hell's anteroom. He saw two bloated forms, barely recognisable as a man and a woman, propped upright in high backed chairs. He saw white-grey skin stretched and tinted to a pale merlot with lividity where the blood had pooled post mortem. He smelled gases that escaped from the forms, yielding odours that were at once sweet and sour, foul and foetid. His own blood, fresh and berry red, ran into his mouth, yet he made no attempt to move away or to cry out, for he was utterly transfixed, like a pinned prize butterfly newly added to the collection.

Damien Roth had been moving around somewhere behind him. The only sound was his rubber-soled shoes on the battered lino.

"You shouldn't worry Mum and Dad like that. Staying out late. Say you're sorry."

Damien pinched him, and then punched him harder than before. Ian Marshall licked at the blood on his lips, on his teeth, and tasted copper. He tried to focus on an ancient television set rather than dwell on what sat beside him.

"Oh no, young fellow my lad, no television for you, not until you've said sorry."

Damien pinched him again and again. "Go on, say it. Say sorry."

"Sorry," he whispered.

"Louder," demanded Damien.

"Sorry," he tried again.

"Now say it like you mean it!"

"I'm sorry!"

"There, that's better. Now you can watch telly for as long as you like, can't he, Mum, Dad?"

Ian Marshall felt the warmth of wool against his neck. Damien was wrapping a scarf around him. The scarf smelled of death.

His Family

Damien Roth stood back and admired his handiwork: mother, father, younger brother, all united in front of the television set, just like a real family should be. There was only thing missing to complete the tableau, and he'd kept it by since he'd found it in the gutter, for he knew it would set things off a treat. From a cardboard box he retrieved the body of a cat, two-day-old road kill. It was partially disembowelled and floppy, but he arranged it tenderly on Audrey Lomax's lap as if it were a prize Persian, and set her dried and flaking hand upon it, stroking her cherished pet.

He sat in the remaining chair, enjoying the company once again of his family. This is how it should be: no fighting, no shouting, no father standing at the foot of your bed waiting to say goodnight in his own special way, no mother spending your Christmas money on making her arm look like a pin cushion, no younger brother who liked to play with matches. Perfect.

And so it was we came across them, this family from beyond hell. I had no gloves. I had to touch him, to lead him away from the scene and steer him into the patrol car, my hand protecting his head. He smelled of Vick's. We had been summoned to do another more exhaustive search, and my partner and I had been instructed to check the upper floors of the old wing, even though we'd been reliably informed that we would find absolutely nothing except a few rusting pieces of hospital equipment.

But what we found instead was Damien, his father, his mother, his younger brother, and the family pet, all sitting before the television set, with Damien himself, wearing a blue striped scarf with his porter's uniform, pouring imaginary tea from a chipped tea pot for them all.

Unfortunately, during the arrest his skull did make contact with the car's doorframe. Damien Roth is awaiting the results of a claim under the Criminal Injuries Compensation Authority

2008, while I remain suspended on full pay pending an investigation.

A SONG, A SILENCE

John Forth

"Cheeky little bastard!"

Harris felt foolish the moment the curse left his lips. For the past six or seven miles he'd been trying to keep a lid on his temper, fingers tightening on the steering wheel, eyes fixed on the rear window of the people carrier blocking the road ahead. The little boy staring back had been innocent enough to begin with, stabbing his tongue out at Harris, pressing his nose against the glass until it squashed flat like a piglet's. Harris had tried to ignore him, concentrating his attention on the twist of the country road – too narrow to risk overtaking – but the monotony of the fields forced his eyes back again and again to the grinning face. Like an idiot, he'd pulled faces back at the kid, hoping that having coaxed a rise out of him, the little boy would leave him be. But no, that only made things worse. When the boy mimicked an act that he should have been too young to know, Harris blurted out an outraged laugh. If that had been the end of it, there wouldn't have been a problem, but then the kid had decided to show his full range of perverse mimes. For the next set of tedious twists and turns, Harris had been subject to a stream of gestured abuse so foul that he thought about ramming the back of the car just to teach the little shit a lesson.

Were the boy's parents blind, or just apathetic to their spawn's behaviour? Perhaps he should flash his headlights to get their attention – although in the dark there was a danger that he'd startle the driver and find himself responsible for the people carrier veering off the road and into the hedge that lined the broken tarmac. At least that would get the bloody kid out of his face. Why were they letting him hop about in the back like that anyway? One emergency stop and the kid might – with any luck – end up toppling over and breaking his neck. Maybe the parents didn't care. Maybe they were taking him off to a remote grave somewhere. Christ, if only …

In an effort to distract himself, Harris put on the radio. The main stations were fragmented, a jumble of indistinct voices battling and failing to find prominence over one another; the local broadcasts appeared to consist of farming alerts and what sounded like snatches of telephone calls. Switching it off, he glanced down at his mobile phone, which lay on the passenger seat. The signal indicator was down to a sliver of a bar. That in itself was a surprise. This far from the nearest town he'd have expected the phone to be dead.

The boy was still watching him, fingers up in front of his face in a V sign, tongue flicking between them. "Dirty little shit-pipe," Harris shouted, slapping the vinyl steering wheel with one damp palm. The boy, realising he had coaxed a reaction from the man, redoubled his efforts. Harris began to mouth back threats, no longer caring how ridiculous he looked, or whether the boy's parents could see him in the rear view mirror. Either he vented now, or he'd be left fuming all night, and after the sort of day he'd had Harris didn't fancy lying awake all night plotting revenge on a fucking nine-year-old.

Still grumbling, Harris followed the people carrier down the steep slope towards a T-junction. His complaints turned into prayers for the boy and his family to take a right and leave him with a clear run to the main road, but no. The winking orange light was as much of a taunt as the boy's beaming face. Groaning, Harris switched on his own indicator, and swung his car in the people carrier's wake.

The clock on the dashboard flicked once, and the digits changed. Only ten thirty, but it may as well have been three or four in the morning for all the moonlight that made it through the clouds. Not for the first time, he cursed whatever cretin had thought to hold the management team-building session so far from civilisation. "We need to get away from it all," the CEO had said, and Harris had agreed – what else could he do? He would probably have still agreed even if he'd known that the old bastard had planned to summon them out into the middle of nowhere. It wasn't as if he had a choice. He yawned, making no effort to stifle it despite the boy's ever-watching eyes. What time had he needed to get up at that morning? It seemed so long ago he could hardly remember. Another minute ticked away on the clock. His flat – and more pertinently, his bed – had never felt further away.

The broad dome of light on the horizon came without warning, appearing as he pulled the vehicle around another turning and on to the long strip of road leading away from the hills. Services, this far from the motorway? Probably not, but the light might at least indicate a garage or an all-night store. Harris glanced at the child, who had clearly exhausted his repertoire and returned to one of his earlier tricks. Loathe as he was to lose any more time, he made a vow to himself. If the people carrier didn't stop at the garage and allow him past, then he'd stop there himself, grab a sandwich and wait for half an hour until his little nemesis was far, far away.

It took less than ten minutes to reach the garage, Harris hoping all the way that the other vehicle would slow and turn in. No such luck. It was foolish of him to expect a break after everything else that had happened. The people carrier sped past the poorly arranged collection of low buildings without hesitation. Taking a moment to jab a single-fingered gesture at the child, Harris turned on to the forecourt and brought his car to a halt.

If it hadn't been for the lights, Harris might have thought the garage had been abandoned. A single pump sat beside the stump of its long-gone partner, white arc lamps above buzzing and spitting. The main building was mostly dark, save for a small lamp shining near the service window and the muted glow of the sparsely stocked refrigerated shelves. Harris could see no sign of movement. Reluctantly, he stepped out of the car and crossed the overgrown forecourt. In the shadows of the derelict outbuildings, he could see black torpedo shapes scuttling back and forth, and from somewhere distant came the anguished bark of a fox either in heat or pain.

Reaching the service window – the main door would be locked at this time of night – Harris put his face close to the glass and peered in. Beneath the glare of the lamp he could see the till, and beside it a sports newspaper whose coverage consisted mainly of barely clad women posing with whichever bat or ball was used for the game in question. He wondered if perhaps the place was abandoned after all, and squinted to see if he could make out the date on the paper. So intensely was he concentrating on the newsprint that he didn't see the scrawny figure emerge from the doorway at the back of the shop.

The attendant was young, probably no older than seventeen or eighteen, and rake thin. Thick curls topped a long narrow face beset with acne pits. As he shuffled up to the glass, the thin boy scraped at a particularly dense cluster of spots on his cheek, not looking at Harris. When he spoke, his voice was so weak it only just managed to squeeze through the holes in the glass.

"Help you?"

"Are you open?" Harris said, looking around at the ruined garage.

"Lights are on, aren't they?"

"That remains to be seen," Harris said, under his breath. "What have you got to eat in there?"

A spastic twitch jolted the attendant's shoulders, and he gave a vague gesture in the direction of the three or four sandwiches that remained. Harris stared at him. Was it his night to be mocked by children? "I mean what flavours do you have?" he said, voice firming.

"Dunno."

Harris felt his hands clench into fists. "Well, why don't you go and find out. And while you're doing that, I'll fill up the car. You do have petrol in those ... in that pump, I assume?"

The attendant looked back at him with incomprehension, then turned to make his way towards the sandwiches.

Harris stomped back across to the pumps, feeling his fury building again. Great – mocked by one kid through the safety

153

of glass, and now here he was struggling to communicate with another. The attendant was lucky he had a barrier in front of him; otherwise Harris might have stuck the petrol nozzle down his throat. Instead, he settled for jamming it into the side of the car and stood watching the cost tick up on the pump's readout. Behind the windows of the main building, he could see the attendant's lethargic shadow creeping back and forth. If only he could get his hands on the bastard – he'd wring a few words out of him.

The singing must have started while he was filling up the car, but Harris couldn't say for sure. At first he thought he was imagining it; that the slow, lilting tune was nothing more than the ghost of a song he had heard long ago, still floating around his head. But the more he focused on it, the more he came to realise that it was on the air, distant and indistinct, but undeniably tangible.

Returning the nozzle to its holster, Harris stepped away from the car and moved towards the point where the gravel of the forecourt met the thick fringe of field beyond. Placing one hand on a crooked wooden fencepost, he cocked his head to listen. The song swam on the air, in and out of audibility, a tuneless but strangely appealing sound. An urge came over Harris, quite unbidden, to climb the fence and walk off across the fields to find the source of the voice. But the grasslands were flat black pools, and there were no lights on the dark shoulder of the mountains. Still, he felt one foot lifting from the ground and pressing against the taut wire of the fence. It was as if the voice were reaching beneath his arms to lift him up and carry him towards its source. It was ridiculous. The cogent part of his mind was telling him not to be stupid, but still he couldn't help himself. Without understanding his own actions, Harris placed his weight on the fence and prepared to push himself over.

The wire buckled under his foot; the fencepost tilted wildly, dragging him over. Letting out a cry, Harris pulled himself back before he could fall headlong into the field. The stream of curses he followed it with drowned out the song on the air, and by the time he had finished, the singing had stopped.

Harris glanced over his shoulder to see if the attendant was watching, but the distance was too great to tell. After lingering a moment longer to see if he could pick up the sound again, he started back to the service window. As he approached, the young man's grinning face fell into focus.

"Pump one, aye?" said the attendant.

"Funny bugger," Harris said, without mirth. He looked down at the ugly sandwich wrapped in plastic sitting in the tray. "What's that?"

"Chicken or something."

Harris looked at him.

"It's all there is."

Harris grabbed the meal and threw a note into the tray. As he took his change, he couldn't help but ask, "Did you hear that?"

Once again, the attendant looked blank.

"That music …? Just now …?"

Nothing. Unable to believe the kid's ignorance, Harris just glared through the glass for a moment. Then, with a shake of his head, he turned and started back to the car. The night was silent again. Even the vermin that he'd seen earlier had been stilled by the song.

The road ahead was blissfully empty as Harris pulled away from the station. He'd given the people carrier enough of a head start that he was unlikely to catch up with it now. Still, in his impatience to get home, Harris drove faster than he should have on the tight country road. More than anything, he craved the close comfort of the city. There was something about the broad open spaces all around that made him nervous.

There wasn't much further to go. The trees and hedges on either side of the road were sparser now, and the hills and fields less steep. He was hitting the lowlands, on the cusp of reaching civilisation once again. With the end of his journey in sight, and his pint-sized nemesis far away, Harris began to relax. The sky was clearer than it had been earlier, allowing the moonlight to lay its pale hands over the land. To one side was a deep, grassy ravine that ran alongside the road for almost a mile. From out of the darkness loomed tourist signs advertising the ragged gash as a dried-up prehistoric loch, which made Harris laugh. What sort of sad act would want to come all the way up here just to look at a crack in the ground? Fill it up with water again and put a couple of hotels at either end, then it might be worth the drive.

Harris was still indulging in this refurbishment fantasy when he spotted light up ahead. Could it be streetlights? Oh, sweet civilisation! Yes, they were sparingly spaced, but there they stood, sentinels preparing to salute his route to the motorway. Distantly, Harris could see the road widening, and at its far end lay a broad mound that could only be a roundabout island. Further, he thought he could see the lights of a farmhouse along one of the branches stretching away from the roundabout. Although Harris couldn't think why someone would want to live all the way out here, he welcomed the sight nonetheless.

The song came again, quite without warning. Insidious, it whispered through the drone of the engine and wormed its way into the car. It was louder than before, and Harris could more clearly make out the spiralling, soaring notes; the tumbling pitch. Male or female, Harris couldn't tell. The voice had no source. It was on the wind, under his skin; it almost seemed to reverberate along the length of his bones.

Harris felt himself drift again, and clutched tightly at the steering wheel. The sharp and sensible part of his mind realised that if he lost control while in the driving seat the result could be cataclysmic. He shook his head, blinked. His mind sent messages to his foot, telling it to ease off the accelerator and on to the brake, but there was no response. The song was behind him like a great gale, a cold embrace impelling him towards the onrushing island of earth at the centre of the roundabout.

The influence of the voice was so great that Harris almost

didn't notice the people carrier. It sat on the incline of the mound, canted to one side, doors wide as if it had thrown out arms to embrace its fate. The front end was buried in the wig of foliage that topped the island, and all around lay small pieces of debris that looked to Harris like torn clothing. There was no sign of the kid or his parents.

Again, Harris tried to break himself out of the spell of the song. Up ahead two brown tracks of churned-up earth showed where the people carrier had left the road and ploughed up through the thick grass that covered most of the island. Realising that he was heading straight for the point where the tyre marks started, Harris tried to wrestle the wheel to the left or right – anywhere but straight ahead – but either it was locked on course, or his arms refused to obey. His body was rigid, a lifeless dummy loaded into the car and thrust towards obliteration. The only part of his body that was active seemed to be his foot, which was pressing down on the accelerator, harder and harder.

"Oh, Jesus, no."

The song reached its apex as Harris's car struck the concrete lip of the traffic island and leapt up on to the grass. The impact jolted him forward, seatbelt lashing taut across his torso and blasting the wind from his lungs. Wheezing, gasping, the influence of the song momentarily broken, he clutched and jerked the steering wheel to the left. Beyond the windscreen, he saw the world begin to tilt, the people carrier tipping from view, then the motion threw him sideways and his head connected with the side window. There was a crack – the glass or his skull, Harris couldn't tell – and an explosion of light. Then nothing.

For a while ...

*

Either everything hurt, or nothing did. There was no context to allow Harris to say for sure. His entire body pulsed and shuddered, limbs imbued with a strange loose tension, which made him worry that he'd suffered some significant nerve damage. How badly had he been injured? Harris was afraid to open his eyes to find out. He wasn't even sure if he *could* open his eyes. One felt slicked over and gummy, and the other heavy and groggy. Raising his shaking hands, he touched his face, expecting to feel the sharp edges of broken glass embedded there. Thank Christ, there was nothing, but one side of his face was wet and sticky. His head. Of course, he had struck his head against the window.

Wiping the blood from his face, Harris opened his eyes. To his surprise, the windscreen was intact – the view outside a mess of branch and leaf – and the car had remained upright. That hadn't prevented the interior being thrown into chaos, however. The papers he'd had rested on the passenger seat were scattered on the floor amidst CD cases, some of which had broken and spilled their contents. Printouts and plastic lay beneath his feet and across his lap. Harris swept them away and looked around. Where was his mobile phone?

First thing first – he had to get out of the car. There was no smell of petrol, and he couldn't see any sign of fire, but Harris knew the dangers. Fumbling at the seat belt release, he eased the strap across his body, aware of the bite it had left across his torso. As he opened his door he saw for the first time the cracked web his head had left on the window, a broad red spider sitting at its centre. Harris turned his gaze away and swung the door open. He didn't need any reminders about how lucky he had been.

Carefully, Harris swung his legs out and placed them on the slight incline. There was no damage to his body – at least not as far as he could tell – but the shaking had yet to subside, and he found that he was too weak to support himself. Instead, he crawled away from the car for a few feet and then turned to slump on his elbows halfway between where his vehicle lay, and the still corpse of the derelict people carrier.

The skid marks cut into the ground allowed him to trace the

trajectory his car had taken. He had been within seconds of crashing into the other vehicle when he had turned the wheel, and his new path had taken him straight into the thick bush at the top of the mound. Just as well that it was comprised mostly of brittle branches and small trees – if he'd struck anything more resilient then it may well have been the end of him. In a way, the small copse had saved his life.

Strength returning to his body, Harris pushed himself up until he was on his knees, than forced himself to his feet. He thought of returning to his car to see if he could retrieve his phone, but was distracted by the mystery of the people carrier. Closer now, he could see that the debris he'd noticed earlier were indeed items of clothes – a few odd socks, a pair of men's trousers, a brassiere. Had someone's luggage exploded during the crash? If that was what had happened then where was the case? And, more importantly, where was the boy and his family? The car didn't look particularly damaged, so perhaps they had walked off to find help. Hadn't he seen the lights of a house nearby? Harris started to make his way to the top of the mound to see if he could locate it.

As he ascended the slight slope, Harris' thoughts turned to the cause of the crash. He could still hear the song, but now he was sure it was just a trace memory etched on his mind by the trauma of what had happened. Try as he may, Harris could barely comprehend why the music had had such a profound effect on him. It was as if he'd been hypnotised, as if the source of the sound was calling to his very core. For the first time, he wondered if the music had been in his head all along. Maybe he'd suffered some kind of seizure. Weren't your senses supposed to behave strangely before a fit? Harris was sure he'd read that somewhere or other.

Touching the wound on the side of his head, Harris decided that he needed help sooner rather than later.

At the top of the mound, Harris stopped and scanned the surrounding area. There were three roads leading away from the roundabout, including the one extending across the countryside towards the next town and, further on, the city. Fields and forest dominated the landscape, but a little way along the road sat a single dwelling which – judging by the high, corrugated shelters behind – may have once been a farmhouse. A single light shone in a second floor window, and Harris thought that he might have seen someone moving within.

He had just started walking down the far slope of the mound when he heard the sound. At first, he thought the moan was nothing more than wind passing through the foliage, but it soon grew into something more guttural. Harris turned and looked towards the thicket. Had something moved there? He supposed there must be birds and rabbits living on the roundabout, but the noise he'd heard was nothing like any animal he'd ever heard. It had sounded almost human.

Crouching low, Harris peered into the dark centre of the copse. There was something in there, no doubt. Behind the tangle of branches, he saw something long and white lying on the ground. As he watched, it twitched once and then shot into the dark, leaving a slick trail behind.

Some kind of snake? Harris didn't think they came in that size around these parts. Reaching out a hand, he pulled the plant life aside and looked in. The damp patch where the serpent had been lying looked black under the moonlight, and led to what Harris initially thought was a deep patch of shadow, but as his eyes adjusted he soon realised was a deep hole cut in to the earth.

The opening was too large to be a rabbit warren. Harris could have fit in easily without his shoulders touching the side. Confused, he shuffled slightly forward to the edge of the hole and looked inside. The dark was at its deepest within, but as he waited for his eyes to adjust, Harris fancied he could see movement. He leant in further.

The face swimming in the darkness was instantly familiar to Harris. Hadn't he spent the better part of the evening watching it mouth obscenities at him? The boy had nothing to say now, though. His mouth hung slack, tongue rolled back into his throat. His eyes were white and sightless. One side of the boy's head had been caved in, jagged teeth of bone biting through his torn scalp. Harris realised what he'd seen being dragged through the grass. But then who—?

A hand appeared from the darkness behind the boy's head and clawed at the dead face. Despite the dark, Harris could make out the broken and ragged fingernails and the pale, fleshy pallor of the skin. As the first hand pulled the boy further down into the hole, a second reached up towards Harris. Flinching, Harris fell back, his palm splashing down in the slick path he had followed to the hole. Sickened, he scurried away on his hands and feet, a shriek building in his throat.

Fingers appeared above the edge of the warren, stained with the boy's blood. A slim white arm followed each of them, bracing to support whatever was pulling its way out of the ground. Harris struggled to turn and drag himself to his feet, but he could not tear his gaze away from the hole. The top of a head appeared, a thick and unkempt mane of fair hair clotted with dirt and mulch. Uneven lines ridged the forehead. Harris couldn't think what they reminded him of until he saw the eyes – wide and perfectly round. Nausea turned his stomach. They were the glassy, unblinking eyes of something aquatic.

The sight was enough to force Harris to his feet. Giving voice to a scream, he fled down the side of the mound and on to the road. There were no cars, but he wouldn't have paused even if there were. Without looking back, Harris sprinted across the tarmac towards the road leading to the city, and the farmhouse that stood by its side.

The song started again just as he reached the side of the road. Screaming to drown it out, Harris clapped his hands hard over his ears and kept running. If he stopped then that strange sound would take hold of him and lead him back to whatever had made its lair on the roundabout. The aches and pains from the crash were finally asserting themselves on his body. Head down, Harris pushed towards the farmhouse driveway, shouting out for help. Even pausing on the doorstep threatened to be the undoing of him.

The door opened just as Harris reached it, and he sprawled into the hallway. Without looking at his saviour, he began to shout, "Close it. Close it now." Only when he heard the door slam shut did he let his hands fall from his ears.

The singing had stopped. In its place was the sharp tick of the grandfather clock at the end of the hall and the ragged wheeze of Harris's own breathing. When he was able to bring himself under control, Harris put a hand out to grab the corner of an ornamental table to pull himself up. The porcelain fish there toppled and fell as his hand slipped. Harris felt something press a palm against his back to help him up. "Steady there, mate. I've got you."

"Jesus. I'm sorry. I'm sorry." Harris allowed the man to help him to his feet. "There's something out there, on the road."

"Don't worry, man, you're okay now."

Disengaging himself from the other's grip, Harris looked to see who the speaker was. The man was young, in his early twenties, and overweight to the extent that his red T-shirt stretched taut as a second skin. Large glasses were gradually slipping down his long nose, and as Harris watched the young man pushed them back into place. He must have been listening to music when Harris arrived, as he wore a pair of large headphones around the rolls of his neck.

"Thanks, son," Harris said. "You really saved me. The name's Harris. Tony Harris."

"Billy Dean," said the youth. "You come from the roundabout?"

"Yes. Yes! There was music, and I crashed. Did you lock the door? Lock the door. There's something out there."

With a nod, Billy Dean put one arm around Harris's shoulders and coaxed him along the hallway towards the stairs. Face grim and voice low, Dean started to ascend, taking Harris with him. "You look like you've had a bit of a fright, pal. Let's get you rested and then you can tell me all about it. Do you need me to phone an ambulance, or just the AA?"

"The police," Harris said. "You need to phone the police. There's something living out there ... a girl ... but her eyes ... her skin ..."

Billy Dean steered Harris along the top landing. The first door they passed was open slightly, and from within Harris could hear other male voices – two at most – chattering in hushed tones to one another. Dean hurried him on before he had a chance to glance in. Was there anyone else in the house apart from young men? Without knowing why, Harris started to feel uncomfortable.

"Do you live here on your own?" he asked.

"Uh ... no. Me and my, uh, brothers stay here with our parents. But they're out tonight. In town."

At the end of the landing, Billy Dean opened a door that led in to an old-fashioned looking bedroom. A heavy dresser sat against one wall, a stiff-legged single bed by the other. Neither looked like they'd seen much use over the years, so thick was the coating of dust that lay over the room. Apart from those items, there was no other furniture, just a couple of small landscape paintings on the wall above the bed. Heavy canvas curtains covered the window.

"Rest up here, mate," Dean said. "I'll make a phone call for you."

Still dazed from his experience, Harris sat down on the bed and held his throbbing head in his hands. Under his breath, he muttered a thanks to Billy Dean, then, realising that he probably hadn't heard him, spoke louder. When he looked up, however, the younger man had gone, and the bedroom door was closed. Through the wall, he could hear the low murmur of male voices.

Harris lay down.

The roof was cracked and flaking, and in one corner was a web which reminded Harris of the crack he'd received to his head. Probing it with his fingers, he wondered if his experience on the traffic island had been a result of the injury. Christ – what if all he'd seen was the boy and his mother, hurt and trying to crawl to safety? He'd left them behind. Harris cupped his hands over his eyes and let out a long groan. What had he done? Were they still out there? Dying in the cold? The thought made him feel sick, and he sought out a distraction. With nothing else to engage his attention, he stood and crossed to the window. A grey fall of dust drifted over his fingers as he opened the curtains. There wasn't much to see. The rusted sheds were empty save for the crumbling husks of old farm vehicles. At least he *thought* they were farming vehicles – in the gloom one or two of them looked like plain old cars, but that couldn't be right, could it? Troubled, Harris let the curtains fall back. As he turned away from the window, his gaze was drawn to the paintings on the wall.

The first was the sort of Scottish landscape he'd seen dozens of times before; indeed, they'd had several on the walls of the conference room he'd spent most of the day in. Rolling hills, stormy skies; the usual clichés. A long body of grey water dominated the scene, so murky that it may as well have consisted of pure peat. In the centre was a small island, topped by bare trees rendered in simple strokes by the painter. Was there a figure on the island? In the faint light of the room it was impossible to say, but he thought so. There was nothing else that the crude white blob at the centre could be.

The island was the focal point of the second painting, and here there could be no question what the artist was intending to depict. Amongst the skeletal trees stood a girl or young woman, entirely naked, looking out across the frothing waters of the loch. Washed up on the black, pebbled shore were two or three broken wooden boats. The shattered branches beneath the woman's feet were the finest ivory.

Harris looked back to the first painting, at the shape of the slopes which lay behind the loch. He knew this place. He had passed through it earlier that night.

Where was Billy Dean?

The muttering in the next room had stopped, but Harris hadn't heard anyone go back downstairs. Crossing to the door, Harris half expected to find it locked, but the handle turned with ease. The landing was dark, lit only by the sliver of light escaping from the other bedroom. If there was anyone in there, they were silent now. Approaching the door, Harris couldn't help but look in.

The first thing he noticed was the telescope, set on its stand and pointing towards the room's single window. It was not an expensive instrument; in fact it made Harris think of the sort of thing a mother would buy a curious child to placate him – decent enough to encourage his interest, but cheap enough that it could be easily dumped in the back of a cupboard if he grew bored of it. On the windowsill, two pairs of binoculars stood upright and, on the office chair that sat near the telescope, was a digital camera with a wide, hungry looking lens.

Certain that there was no one inside, Harris opened the door and stepped in. Like the other bedroom, this one was sparsely furnished. The bed was little more than a bare frame, and there were no paintings on the flaking walls. But on the floor, a laptop computer and a small home printer sat on a nest of tangled cables, and spread across the uncarpeted boards were printouts of dozens of photographs. A dread weight in his stomach, Harris moved closer, already knowing what he was going to see.

The photographs had all been taken from a single angle, each showing the same curve of earth and thatch of hedge. Most appeared to have been shot at night, although in some there were patches of burnt umber cloud which suggested late evening or daybreak. Harris thought that they were all part of a sequence, until he began to spot the differences between each. The cars, for one thing. Sometimes they were parked at the edge of the roundabout, sometimes they had come to a halt near the summit as Harris had earlier. Each had been left in the same state – doors open, no sign of the driver or any passengers – but every single one was a different make and model to the last. The people carrier had not been the first vehicle to come a cropper on the traffic island.

Disgusted at the implications, Harris swept his hand across the nearest set of photographs, brushing them under the bed. In doing so, he only uncovered others, and these were the worst of all. The figure – the girl – he'd seen crawling from the pit featured in all of them, revealed to the world. Bare skin the colour of the moon, she dominated each photo. Mostly she crouched in or around the broken vehicles that had washed up on her concrete shore, lank hair hanging over her face as she ransacked the interiors, looking for God only knew what. In others she was crawling down at the edge of the roundabout island, one hand reaching out to touch the tarmac as if to check that it was as solid as it appeared. Those photos sent a shudder through Harris, but they were not the worst. No, the most terrible ones were those where the occupants of the vehicles were still visible. They were in the girl's clutches mostly, almost shapeless as they were dragged from their cars and across the grass. But in others they were clearly still aware, trapped in their seats, mouths and eyes wide. In one, the girl knelt near a blurred shape, her arm high and in motion, clutching something that she appeared to be bringing down with some violence.

Harris stood too quickly, a dark haze encroaching on his vision. Putting out a hand to steady himself, he found only the telescope, which twisted on its tripod and sent him stumbling. He came to a halt by the window, gripping the sill. Outside, the road pointed straight to the roundabout, where Harris's car remained. Atop the vehicle's roof, just visible over the rise, lay the figure. From this distance, it was as much an indistinct smudge as it had been in the ugly paintings in the next room, but Harris could see it moving. Curiosity conquering his fear for a moment, he stepped back and put his eye to the telescope.

It took only a few seconds to focus on the girl. She lay on her front, legs kicking idly in the air like an adolescent, head and shoulders hidden beneath her thick fall of hair. There was no violence in her at that moment, just the fidgeting boredom of youth, but on her arms Harris could see long, dark streaks that still ran wet, and dotting her body were several spots of varying sizes which now and then would slide across the gentle curves of her body leaving thin black lines behind them.

Despite himself, Harris felt a twinge of desire. It did not last long, however. The more he looked at the girl, the less convincing her imitation of humanity became. The fingers which she used to comb through her hair looked held together by webs of skin and what he had mistaken for nails earlier seemed more to be a bony growth jutting from the ends of each digit. Her flesh, virgin white on first glance, came to remind him of the underside of a trout or another fish, and he imagined how it must feel to the touch – yielding and blubbery, rough with flaking scales. The girl looked up, her hair falling away from her face. In the moment before he snapped back from the telescope, Harris was sure that he'd seen three useless folds of red and exposed skin just beneath the girl's jawline, fluttering in the memory of water passing through, but he did not want to look back. Did not want to risk seeing those terrible, undersea eyes again.

That was enough. Harris stumbled towards the door and on to the landing. He had to get out of there and as far along the road as possible. He would run all the way back to the city, even if it took all night and his lungs exploded along the way. At that moment, a coronary at the side of the road was preferable to another moment within the range of the creature on the roundabout and her terrible voice. Reaching the top of the stairs, he prayed that no one else would come along the road; not for their safety – Harris couldn't care less about that – but to ensure that the singing didn't start again until he was far, far away.

Billy Dean was waiting at the bottom of the stairs, his two companions close behind.

They were all of a type – hair long and greasy, T-shirts marked with food stains and tiny circular burns. Each wore a pair of headphones similar to those he'd seen around Dean's neck when he'd first came to the house; large enough to encompass the entire ear, the edges cushioned to prevent any sound from escaping, or from getting in. Only now did Harris notice that there were no leads hanging from the headphones, nothing to connect them to a speaker with. Embarrassment joined his anger and fear.

"Get out of the way."

Billy Dean took a single step up the stairs. Harris saw that he was carrying something long and solid in his left hand. When he spoke back, his voice was raised, although there was no anger in it. Of course, Harris realised, the youth was speaking to hear himself over his headphones.

"We're sorry, mate," Dean said. "Really, really sorry."

"Move!"

"It's just, there can't be any witnesses. If they find out about her then they'll take her away from us, and we can't have that."

"Shift!"

Dean kept coming. "I'm really sorry, man."

Realising he had no choice, Harris kicked out at Dean, sending him sprawling with a squeal down the stairs. While the other two men were still in shock, Harris leapt down after him, grabbing the post at the bottom of the stairs and swinging himself in to the hallway. The door was closed, but he didn't think that Billy Dean had locked it earlier. Surely he was due at least a bit of luck that evening.

Something solid struck the back of his neck, just where his spine touched his skull. A flash of stars appeared before his eyes, and then something hit his knees – the floor. Moaning, crawling, Harris attempted to hold on to his consciousness, but the lights sparking in front of him grew more agitated the harder he tried. Heavy footsteps came rushing up behind him, and he was struck again, on the back of the head this time. Now his arms were crumpling, and the lights were blinking out one by one. There was another strike, but it may as well have been the echo of a drumbeat from a mile away or more. His face struck the floor, which was softer than he'd expected. So soft, that he felt himself being sucked down, and into the earth below.

*

Harris awoke twice after that, both times in complete darkness. The first time, he was tangled up in a sack of rough material, being dragged across hard, cold ground. He tried to buck and kick his way free, but both his hands and feet were tied and he was unable to free himself from his bounds. Distantly, he could hear the song, softer than before, but no less persuasive. He felt himself tiring, lulled back into unconsciousness, and his struggles stopped. Within moments, there was nothing but the song.

The second time, he was free of the sack, and beneath him the earth was damp and irregular. His hands were unbound, but when he tried to reach out he found that he remained incapable of moving more than a few inches. The song was at its quietest, but closer than ever. It came from somewhere a little distant from Harris's feet, and from the same direction he could hear a soft snuffling, the rattle of bones.

He may have lain there for hours before she finally came to him, moving through the dark to his side unseen, cooing in his ear. When her touch came, the sensation was everything he feared, and when she opened her mouth to feed – wide, so much wider than should have been possible – Harris began to wish that the song would never stop.

THE MAN WHO HATED WASTE

Marc Lyth

It wasn't his fault. The man had just stepped out into the road and he didn't have a chance. All right so he was going a bit too quickly but the guy should have stayed on the pavement. Now Stevie Walsh had a dent in the car that would cost a fortune to fix, a cracked windscreen and there was a guy on the tarmac who didn't seem to be moving.

Stevie stopped the car and cursed. He was on his way back from the recycling centre – the third run of the day. That's why he was rushing; he had too much to do. He hated waste and made sure he recycled everything. He had another two runs to make and the centre closed in an hour. Damn it! It looked like that was going to have to wait till tomorrow. He got out of the car and opened the boot. There was a large blanket folded neatly next to the large stack of plastic bin bags. Stevie lined the boot quickly with the bin bags and removed the blanket before he walked over to the body on the ground behind the car.

It was indeed dead. There wasn't much blood, but the neck had twisted into an impossible shape and the eyes were open and glassy. Stevie cursed again and laid the blanket next to the corpse. He thanked his time spent in the gym recently as he rolled the body onto the blanket before wrapping it and lifting it into the car boot. Lucky this had happened on the way back. If it had happened on the way there, he wouldn't have had room.

Ten minutes later he was home and the car locked securely in the garage. Stevie started by clearing his worktable, he carried the bundles of old newspapers out of the back door of the garage, past his two compost heaps and into the shed where he placed them next to the broken up wardrobe he was saving for bonfire night and the stacks of old clothes waiting to go down to the Salvation Army depot.

Returning to the garage, he pulled his number 4 toolbox (Light Cutting Equipment) from under the workbench and opened it. The Stanley knife was there and three fresh blades. He tested the blade that was in it and switched it for a new one. Next he found his favourite gallon containers and a pair of funnels. He'd never done this before but he had a basic knowledge of anatomy so it couldn't be too difficult.

He lifted the body from the boot and placed it on the worktable. Even with his time in the gym, it was starting to feel quite heavy. It was too wide for the table and the arms dangled either side. Perfect, thought Stevie as he placed the gallon containers under each of the arms. He then took the funnels and placed them in the containers before putting the hands of the corpse inside the funnels themselves.

He now took the Stanley knife with its lovely fresh blade and slit both the corpse's wrists. The blood started flowing but only slowly.

Once more Stevie cursed, he was on a timetable here. Things needed to be done within certain timescales or so he understood. Remembering his first aid training he ripped open the corpse's shirt, placed the palm of his right hand over the back of his left, interlaced the fingers, located the point midway between the nipples and started CPR on the corpse.

That was better. As he pumped the heart, the wounds on the wrists spurted the blood more quickly into the containers. After fifteen minutes of pumping, Stevie was content that he'd squeezed as much as he could out of the corpse. It was now even whiter than it had been and the containers were both nearly three quarters full. He'd done well with that part of the task. Stevie wiped the sweat from his forehead and sealed the containers before putting them in the fridge.

This would make the next job much less messy as well. He loosened the corpse's trousers and pulled them down slightly, just enough to reveal the pubic hair but not the genitals. There needed to be some dignity left in death. He then retrieved the Stanley knife and made an incision from the trachea to the pubic bone, followed by another cut from shoulder to shoulder.

The man he'd killed had been quite young and fit and there was little to no body fat as he peeled back the flaps of skin across the dead man's chest. The smell hit instantly and Stevie nearly vomited. He should have expected that. He opened the cupboards labelled 'Cleaning Materials – Additional' and removed a number three sized facemask before returning to his task.

To gain better access to the organs in the lower body Stevie made further cuts across the hipbone and peeled the skin fully off the dead man's torso. The prize organs were there behind the ribs – the lungs and the heart. He tried to lift the ribs out of the way but they wouldn't budge. This was something else he hadn't thought of. Obviously the sternum wasn't hinged to the clavicle so it wasn't a straight lift.

For the fifth time today, Stevie found himself cursing. He took two pounds fifty from his pocket and put it in the swear box by the kitchen door. The recycled label on the swear box was peeling. He would need to fix that later. Meanwhile he busied himself by digging his smallest bolt cutters out of his number 1 toolbox (General Use).

As he turned to face the corpse, bolt cutters in hand, he had a thought. How could he be so stupid? He ran to the kitchen and retrieved his freezer boxes, throwing his entire stock of ice into one and several bags of frozen vegetables into the other. He also grabbed some food bags and a couple of carrier bags. Stevie hoped they'd be clean enough for the job in hand.

He returned to the body on the worktable and started work on the ribs. Several were already broken from the CPR and he was able to snap them off and throw them into a neat pile behind him, they would be good for the dog later on. The rest he worked at with the cutters, trying not to damage the tissues behind.

After a few minutes he stopped. He really was going about this the wrong way. He opened his number 3 toolbox (Hammers) and selected a middle-sized claw hammer. Then he unrolled his wrap full of chisels and spent a few moments in thought before selecting a one-and-a-half centimetre chisel, rolling the wrap back up and returning it to the chisel drawer.

He returned to the body and applied the chisel to the clavicle instead. This gave way easily – one side must have been damaged in the accident as it only needed one tap before it snapped completely – and he was able to lift out the entire sternum with the ribs and broken collarbone attached.

Now he had full access to the internal organs he set to work with the Stanley knife, carefully removing first the heart and lungs before bagging them and placing them carefully in the freezer boxes.

As he worked, Stevie quietly sang 'Staying Alive'. The words faded though as he grew more engrossed in his task and he struggled to retrieve what he guessed was a kidney from behind the intestinal cavity. This was really quite fascinating once you got started. Once the organ was removed, he took up a saw and started sawing in time with the Bee Gees tune that was stuck in his head.

After half an hour or so he'd retrieved all the organs he thought were usable. The eyes had popped as he'd tried to remove them, which had disappointed him, but he had a large selection of bits in his freezer boxes now. It had been a good day so far. He loaded them into the back of the car and fetched the gallon jugs from the fridge. These he placed next to the boxes and shut the boot.

He looked at what was left of the body. The muscle tissue he could feed to the dog later – he didn't think it appropriate to eat it himself – but he couldn't think of a use for the intestines yet. There were so much of them. Surely they must be good for something.

He wondered if they could be used for an organic cable once they dried. He could use the contents of the lower intestine on one of his compost heaps. That much was certain. He would sort that out when he got back home later. For now he had an urgent errand to run.

*

Janice had worked at the blood transfusion centre for several years and loved her job. This was one place where all the members of the public who came through the door were decent people who wanted to help. It almost broke her heart when she had to turn people away, but that was the nature of the job and she was always so sympathetic with the rejects, they couldn't ever find it in their hearts to be angry with her for turning them down.

She'd been on duty since nine o'clock in the morning and was looking forward to going home. As much as she loved the job, some days were too long and this was one of them. It was nearly half-past five and the place was nearly empty. She could relax now and surf the internet as long as she was discreet. She opened her favourite shopping site and typed in 'Purple dress' then sat back and tried to make her choice from the dozens that appeared on the screen in front of her.

"I've got a present for you!" a voice with a jovial Irish lilt suddenly sounded in front of her.

She looked up and saw a middle-aged man wearing a leather jacket over what might have been a blue shirt once before it had been apparently soaked in blood and other substances that she couldn't even guess at. From the smell that hit her like the heat from a blast furnace, they were organic fluids but that was as much as she wanted to know.

The man placed two gallon containers on the desk in front of her, the red liquid inside sloshing noisily. He grinned at her, his slightly greying temples flecked with more blood where he'd failed to wash his face properly. "Where do you want it?" he asked.

Janice stared at the man in front of her. This was something she hadn't expected to see when she came in this morning.

She wished she worked at the hospital reception where they had a panic button under the desk. This was considered a low risk position so they hadn't been given that type of security. She knew she was going to have to deal with this herself.

"We have a fridge over there," she said, amazing herself with her calmness. "I'll call one of my colleagues over to give you a hand if you like."

"That'd be grand," said Stevie with a grin on his face. "Here, I've got a lot of bits in the back of the car that you guys might be able to use, can I drop them here or should I take them up to the hospital?"

"Bits ...?" Janice was certain she didn't want to hear the answer to her question, which had slipped out automatically.

"Oh you know, the usual, inside bits, heart, lungs, kidneys and the like." Stevie's grin widened.

"Oh right ..." Janice's previous certainty had been confirmed. "I think we can probably take them here for you. If you'd like to wait over there we can get someone to help you with it all." She somehow managed to smile widely at the man in front of her although she suspected it could turn into a rictus grin if she held it too long. "We're really very grateful for your help," she added.

Stevie took his gallon containers, moved to the waiting area and sat down, reading a second-hand paperback book he fished out of his coat pocket. Janice breathed a sigh of relief and reached for the telephone.

*

Stevie barely spoke at his trial, except, that is, to mutter constantly under his breath, "Ungrateful bastards, they say they're desperate for people to give blood but you bring in two cartons full and look what happens – the ungrateful bastards!" over and over.

He would have owed his swear box a small fortune if he'd had it with him.

SWAN SONG

David A. Riley

Bennett shuddered with revulsion.

Sat on the park bench like a pair of old scarecrows rescued from a refuse dump, the couple made his flesh crawl. They were old, filthy, dressed in clothes that were dropping to pieces. Tramps. That was what we used to call them, Bennett thought. In the good old days when you could still call a spade a spade. What did they call them now, with all their PC crap? Bag people? Still too close to the truth probably. Homeless? Bennett hated that word. It sounded like someone should pity them, not despise or hate.

Bennett grimaced. He could smell them from here, still yards away from them. People like that shouldn't be allowed in the park, polluting it with their vile presence. Why didn't the council recruit guards to keep scum like these two out so that proper people, *decent* people, could enjoy it in peace?

Bennett glared. Somewhere inside their rags he knew they would have bottles of alcohol hidden away. A man and what passed, he supposed, for a woman, both of them getting on, like a pair of geriatric mummies, all skin and bone. Neither of them looked as if they had washed in years; ingrained filth dulled their skin.

Bennett thrust his hands deep inside his overcoat pockets as if he wanted to keep as much of his flesh protected from contamination as possible. His fingers itched. In a properly organised society scum like these would be shot. In his imagination he could visualise doing it. Two headshots, that's all it would take, before their carcasses were carted off to some kind of communal grave to be sown with quicklime and covered in dirt.

Bennett had a vivid imagination.

Though divorced, childless, a self-confessed misogynist, he never felt lonely. A group of cronies at the pub in which he spent most of his nights looked on at him in admiration. They admired the erudite tone of his wit with an awe that tickled his vanity. Once, years ago, he had been a schoolteacher. He had been forced, though, to take early retirement. He had been a good teacher too, even if he did ruffle a few feathers. Not like these namby-pambies nowadays who let their pupils do whatever they liked, leaving school with no more idea of good grammar than some Johnny-come-lately from Wogga-Woggaland. Bennett had known how to keep discipline. There had been no slouchers in his classes. No fidgetters. No cheek.

Bennett's eyes bored into the couple. He expected they would stay transfixed to that bench till they'd guzzled whatever they'd brought with them, then sneak away to buy some more – or steal it.

With an effort of will, Bennett walked past.

With any luck they would be gone tomorrow and he could enjoy his stroll through the park in peace.

The next day, though, they were there again. This time they had brought a flask and a plastic box of sandwiches, lying between them on the bench as if they were having a God damned picnic. Now and then one of them threw a handful of crumbs across the tarmacadammed path for the birds. A flock of pigeons were already pecking at them.

Bennett grimaced. Pigeons were another of his pet hates. They were no better than rats. Feathered vermin. Typical that the old couple should be feeding them.

"Excuse me," Bennett said. He stopped in front of them, regimentally ramrod. The steel ferrule of his rolled umbrella tapped the ground for emphasis. "There's a by-law against doing that." He flicked his hand at the crumbs scattered across the path. "No feeding. You could be fined," he said.

For a moment there was a look of incomprehension in the old couples' faces as they stared up at him. The man's mouth, purple with some kind of growth, like a rope of vein running under his lips, part hidden in stubble, moved into a smile. Bennett felt unsure about it. Was it threatening, half-witted, or

177

an attempt to placate him?

Unused to uncertainty, Bennett nodded his head in an affirmative gesture. "They take it seriously," he said. "There are notices all around the park." Somehow, he realised, he sounded defensive, as if he needed to justify his admonition, even though neither of the old couple had said anything yet. Just that stupid smile from the man, that meant what? Anything? Nothing? Bennett would have preferred a straightforward argument. That he could cope with. That he would have relished. That he knew he would have won. What he could not deal with was this incomprehensible smile. He felt intimidated by it, though he failed to understand why.

"Just be warned," Bennett said after a moment's silence, abhorring himself for it, knowing that he would run over what he had said – or failed to say – the rest of the day, dissatisfied with it. It was something he was not used to experiencing. Inadequacy was anathema. It showed weakness, lack of moral backbone, and cowardice. Things he despised.

He was still seething when he reached the Red Pheasant, a public house across from the main gates into the park. Although he didn't normally drink so early in the day, he felt the need for one now. A stiff brandy to steady his nerves. That was the ticket. Something to take his mind of those scumbags.

"Make it a large one, landlord." He rested his arms on the well-polished bar.

"You look as if you need it." The landlord's world-weary sack of a face had seen too many late nights and not enough sleep.

Bennett growled. "It angers me when people abuse our parks."

"Vandals? I hadn't heard of any trouble."

Bennett shook his head. "A couple of old tramps. Sat like the King and Queen of Sheba. You'd think they owned the place." Bennett frowned; he could feel the landlord's eyes stare at him as he handed him his brandy.

"Wouldn't be a man and a woman?"

Bennett bridled at the man's hushed tone.

"As it happens, yes. Customers of yours?"

The man shook his head, laughing. "You wouldn't find them here, oh no. Not that I'd want them."

"Of course not," Bennett said, wondering. He could sniff the landlord had more to say. Bennett had a nose for nuances, developed over years of dealing with two-faced, duplicitous children. "What do you know about them?"

The landlord leaned over the bar with a conspiratorial air, even though the only other customers were sitting around a table at the far end of the room, too far away to hear. "They're not what you think." The man tapped the side of his nose. "Some say they're worth a friggin' fortune. I wouldn't know about that. But they're well off, that's for sure. How rich?" He shrugged in a gesture that reminded Bennett of a Jewish comedian. "They live in one of those Edwardian villas down Maple Road. It used to belong to the old man's father. In a bit of a state now, I believe."

Bennett frowned. "They're rich?" Somehow this made him dislike the couple even more. They had less reason to be as they were. What kind of degenerates were they? Dropouts? Hippies?

"I'll have another brandy, landlord." Bennett passed him his glass. He felt he might need lubrication to get the brain cells working on what he'd heard. "Have one yourself," Bennett said. There was a smile on his lips that was foxy and cruel. Might as well see what the landlord had to say about that pair. The more he knew about them the better.

An hour later, Bennett left the pub. He knew he had drunk too many brandies and would suffer later. But it had been worth it.

"They used to be great philanthropists, you know," the landlord had said. "Caused a bit of a kafuffle, though, which brought it to an end. That was when they ran a refuge of sorts in town for homeless people."

"Appropriate enough," Bennett said. "They dress like a pair

of vagabonds."

The landlord laughed, perhaps dutifully. "That was before I took over this pub. I didn't live round here then so I only know all this from hearsay. It was around the time I moved here that there was a bit of a scandal." He leaned closer, his breath a tad too close to Bennett's face, but for once he ignored this. "They used to take some of these homeless back to their house, give them a bed to sleep in, fed and clothed them, then sent them on their way with enough money to start a new life. That's what they claimed. Word was, though, that some of these buggers were never heard of again." The landlord shrugged. "You could say why should they? Most of them probably slipped to their old ways again. End of story. Trouble was one of their progenies was different. He wasn't a dropout who'd made a mess of his life or been kicked out by his parents. He came from a good family, had gone to university and almost completed his degree when he had a nervous breakdown. Went right off the rails. Abandoned university and disappeared. His parents were frantic to find him. Thought something bad must have happened to him. The police had photos of him on TV. There were articles in the papers. His parents even hired private detectives to track him down. He was finally traced here. He wrote home to his parents. Just a postcard, if I remember right, to say he'd met some people who were helping him." The landlord winked. "You can guess who."

Bennett nodded his head as expected, wondering when the blasted man would cut to the chase.

"Anyway, the lad's parents contacted the couple and asked about their son. Left weeks ago, they were told. Have no idea where he is now. That's what they said. Trouble was, no one had heard or seen him since that postcard. Well, that was it. A proper shit storm erupted, if you'll pardon the French. The police got a search warrant and for days the house was screened off as they went through it like a dose. Dug up the garden. Made a right proper mess of it, they did. I heard tell every floorboard inside was lifted. Even walls were knocked through in case there were hidden chambers."

"And?" Bennett asked when the landlord paused to replenish their drinks.

"Not a sausage. No trace anywhere. No trace of anything suspicious at all. Red faces all round." The landlord smirked. "Not that this did the couple much good. Gossip was they might have buried the lad's body on the moors somewhere. Too much about their odd lifestyle came out in the press. No one had known till then they'd been into the occult. That all came out, with photos of statues and stuff in their house they'd bought from all over the place. Leaks about some of the books they had on black magic and stuff like that didn't help, of course. There were all sorts of rumours suddenly, most of them probably a load of old bollocks, but shit sticks, doesn't it?"

Purposefully Bennett strode towards the park. By the time he reached the bench they'd occupied earlier the couple had gone. Back to their villa, no doubt, resenting the idea that they could live in the kind of grandeur he'd had described while all he could afford, after a bad divorce and a reduced pension from the Education Authority, was a maisonette. Life was so bloody unjust. If there was a God, He was a fickle, hardhearted bastard, unfair and perverse. Otherwise degenerate scum like the Huntingtons would never be allowed to live in a house like that. Work all your life, scrimp and save, slave to pound what knowledge you could into ungrateful minds week after miserable week, and what was your reward? The answer gnawed at Bennett's bowels like an incurable cancer; he felt tears of frustration in the corners of his eyes.

It just wasn't fair.

It wasn't fair at all.

*

Bennett spent a sleepless night, vexed by thoughts of the couple, as a result of which he was late getting up in the morning. His head ached from the brandies he'd drunk in the

Red Pheasant – and from more he'd drunk back home, staring at the bars of his electric fire. The crisp air helped to clear his head when he ventured out. If nothing else he had his health. He could still do a brisk walk around the better parts of town. Whether it helped his peace of mind to gaze at houses he could no longer afford, he was not sure, though it did him good to feel as if he belonged amongst them, not the one bedroom rabbit hutch he rented. His divorce had left a few thousand in the bank, but nowhere near enough to buy a house of his own. What money he had would see him out if he took care. Though, damn it, he knew this just wasn't really good enough. He had worked all his life and should have been able to spend his remaining years with enough money to splash out on luxuries if he wanted to. The only pleasure left was the occasional Martell he would buy at the supermarket along with his groceries. And the four or five nights he spent each week at the pub.

Although Bennett knew he should have avoided going there, he could not help it. Walking past the end of the park, he carried on towards Maple Road, with its large, stone-built Edwardian villas, erected during an era of ostentation. Bennett loved buildings from that period. He could have lived during those golden years before the First World War with equanimity. It was his ideal time – before socialism spoilt it all.

His heart grew heavy as anger rose in his throat. Bennett stopped in disbelief at the large, sandstone gabled house, knowing it had to be the one that belonged to the couple. From the weathered varnish on its otherwise splendid door and window frames to the dilapidated shrubs that filled the surrounding garden, it stood out from its neighbours. Sun-bleached curtains were drawn at most of the windows and it looked abandoned, an eyesore compared to the rest of the houses here.

The filthy scum! How could they?

Bennett felt the injustice more keenly still.

As he stood at the rusting cast-iron gate he could hear music. Old pop music, sixties stuff, just what he would have expected. A Wagnerian, Bennett still recognised it. 'Nights in White Satin'. Overrated, degenerate trash, just perfect for a pair of ancient hippies, high on drugs.

Now that he had seen the house Bennett returned home, his feelings in turmoil. They were still in that state when he went to the pub that night. The Foxhill was quiet but at least 'Pinky' Pinkerton and Sam Nedwell were already there. Bennett took his whisky and water to their table.

A retired accountant, Pinky was treasurer for his local Conservative Party Association and a staunch admirer of Bennett's wit. His sallow face and downturned mouth would twist like rubber whenever he chuckled at one of Bennett's blistering comments. The stem of a pipe stuck out of the top pocket of his sports jacket. A self-made businessman, who Bennett knew had never been quite as successful as he tried to make out, Sam Nedwell was red-faced and portly. Sporting a pale cream Armani suit too many years out of date, it was already starting to look a tad grubby at the cuffs. Bennett had known both men since their schooldays.

"What's troubling you?" Sam asked in his blunt no nonsense way.

Bennett downed half his whisky and pulled his face. He told them about the tramps in the park.

"Down-and-outers, eh?" Pinky said with a knowing nod.

"Bloody no good fucking drop outs," Sam retorted.

The three men shook their heads.

"But rich." Bennett looked at his friends in turn. "Filthy rich."

"Bastards."

"All inherited," Bennett said, dismissively. "Never earned a penny of it themselves. Had it left to them by the old man's father, who's probably turning in his grave right now."

"Spinning, more like" Sam said. "It's stuff like this makes me glad I've no sprogs to squander what's left of my money when I pop my clogs," though Bennett and Pinky knew to the contrary. Sam had sown more than his fair share of wild oats in the distant past. In his younger days he had been a bit of a lady's man, not that anyone looking at the broken veins littering the cratered knob of his drinker's nose would think that now.

"If they keep feeding those pigeons, you should report them," Pinky said.

Sam shook his head. "They'd get nothing worse than a warning. What good's that?"

"Not good enough, that's what. I want to do more than that," Bennett said. "They're a disease."

"You know what you have to do about them." Sam's watery pale blue eyes stared into his. "Diseases, I mean, old man." he added the grunt of a laugh more pig-like than human.

Pinky frowned. "Inoculate against them?"

Even Bennett laughed this time, having caught Sam's gist. "Eradicate them."

"Like that advert on TV," Sam said. "You know the one? It's got those blasted germs all wallowing around in the toilet bowl. In goes the bloody cleaning stuff, whatever it is, and they burst apart, bloody well killed, the lot of 'em." He leaned back, laughing.

"My wife wouldn't watch any channel but the BBC," Pinky said. "I still don't. Haven't seen an advert in years."

"You don't know what you're missing." Sam wiped tears from his eyes. "Better than the programs half the time."

"Perhaps that's why Pinky's wife would only watch the beeb," Bennett said.

Pinky laughed, his jaundiced face contorting with delight. "Got you there, Sam. Scotched you, you old reprobate."

Sam snorted. "You're probably right. Might be why I spend more time here." He raised his beer in mock salute.

"What do we do about the tramps?" Pinky said, cocking an eye at Bennett.

"What do you mean *do?*" Sam's face became serious again.

"It's years since we did anything like that, if that's what you mean."

"Ten years at least," Bennett said. He didn't need to say more. Starting in their mid-twenties, Bennett and Pinky fresh from university, Sam on his way to his first fortune, ducking and diving, they had been drawn into radical politics "so far to the right even Attila the Hun was out of sight" Bennett used to phrase it. The spark was when Sam had broken a picket line and an angry mob of strikers had beaten him up. He was making a huge profit supplying a firm with raw materials to help blacklegs keep production going. Lorry drivers had refused to pass the pickets, but Sam owned his own vehicle and had been offered umpteen times the going rate for what he was taking in. The three friends had always been close at school, ganging up on anyone who tried to pick on them. Bennett, rubbed raw at being forced to join a teacher's union, had been the most vociferous in Sam's defence. Pinky had already gone through half a dozen right-wing parties by this time, most of which would have got him barred from membership of the Conservatives for life. It had not taken much to persuade the three to retaliate against the men who attacked Sam, finding out where they lived and paying each of them a late night visit. Balaclava clad and armed with baseball bats they had broken several arms and legs and cracked a few heads before lying low. They had been careful to make sure they left no clues as to whom they were and no one, even to this day, had ever pointed a finger at any of them.

Encouraged by their success, they had carried out other 'commando raids' over the years, targeting anyone who made life hard for any of them. It had worked well. Difficult colleagues at school had been reduced to physical and psychological wrecks, sometimes quitting the profession. Sam's business rivals had found life less than rosy if they infringed too much, while Pinky enjoyed it for what it was, an opportunity to wreak violence, safe in the knowledge they were all too clever to get caught – and too respectable to be suspected. Pinky had an edginess that would have shocked his clients, none of whom would have ever imagined that their sallow-faced accountant had such a streak of sadism in him: it was sometimes so severe, in fact, the others had to rein him in, even though they were almost as bad themselves. If they hadn't, though, they would have had more than four deaths on their hands by now.

"You're not going soft on us, Pinky?" Sam said, breaking the silence.

Pinky had large fists, which he rested on the table. They would have made him a formidable boxer if he had gone in the ring, but that was not what interested him. Broken knuckles bore testament to the faces he had enjoyed reducing to bloody ruins, far beyond what any pugilist would have been allowed to go even in his day.

"The spirit's willing," Pinky said with a sigh of regret. "I'm not so sure about the flesh."

"Don't I know it?" Sam grimaced. "The quack's told me to watch my blood pressure. It's sky high. Says I should take it easy; cut back on alcohol, would you believe!" He emptied his glass with a flourish of contempt at the thought.

"We're none of us getting any younger," Bennett said. "The days of taking on all and sundry at the dead of night have long since passed."

"I'll drink to that. Or will when I get a refill." Sam glanced at Pinky, whose round it was.

Bennett drew them in over the table. "Perhaps we should end with a swan song." He smiled at his friends.

"The tramps?" Sam grinned with appreciation. "Degenerate old bastards, ripe for the picking. They'd deserve what they get."

"Why not?" Pinky said. He grinned too, and Bennett wondered if his friend was thinking how far they would let him go this time.

This *last* time.

Satisfied at the outcome, Bennett said, "I'll reconnoitre the place. See what's what."

"Why bother?" Sam asked. "If they're like you've described, let's just go in and deal with them."

Pinky nodded his agreement.

Bennett sighed, though he was pleased at their enthusiasm.

*

It was dark when they set out. Fog blurred the light from the streetlamps, suiting their purpose. Bennett preferred to be seen by as few people as possible. Midweek, there were not many late night revellers as they walked past the edge of the park, its gates locked hours ago. They hurried by. Bennett could feel the frost in the air seep through his coat. Not much further now, though. Already he could see the turning to Maple Road.

A car drove past, gone within seconds. Bennett knew its occupants would hardly have noticed them; even if they did, they wouldn't remember.

Soon he was standing outside at number twelve, its shambolic garden unmistakable in the gloom. There were lights behind the downstairs curtains and, standing at the gate once more, Bennett could again hear music inside. More sixties trash, as distinctive as joss sticks or the sickly stink of marihuana. He told Pinky and Sam to wait till he had gained access.

As his friends stepped back into the darkness of the privets, holding their balaclavas, Bennett gripped the top of the garden gate and swung it open. Striding to the door he grabbed hold of the brass knocker and pounded it hard. Echoes bounced back at him.

Moments later the music dimmed inside and he heard a muffled conversation. A light came on behind the door, before its locks were turned. The door opened and a thin, querulous-looking face peered out; hair hung in a halo on either side of it.

"We spoke yesterday." Bennett's voice sounded oily even to him. "I thought I'd call to apologise." He put on his best smile.

"I think I spoke harsher than I should."

The man smiled at him as he let the door swing open.

"Alicia, we have a visitor."

Bennett was shocked at the old man's voice. It was a dismal whisper that made him shiver with revulsion. Worse, the smell inside the vestibule was a rank mixture of vegetable decay, dead rodent and dust. There was a disturbing sweetness mingled with it, reminding Bennett of dry rot. This was so intense that he began to worry how safe the building was. Again he noticed the purplish red vein below the old man's mouth, though it seemed lower this time. The skin around it looked raw as if it had been bleeding. Bennett curled his lip in disgust.

"Come in, come in." The old man wafted Bennett to enter. He wore a threadbare cardigan that hung full of holes from his scrawny shoulders. As his hand urged Bennett in, it was as if his cardigan was woven out of spiders' webs and was ready to fall to pieces.

Bennett slid past, trying to avoid any physical contact. The man revolted him even more inside the thick atmosphere of the house, and for a moment Bennett wondered whether he had made a mistake in coming here, for all he despised the repulsive couple and hated what they had done to this house.

Beyond the vestibule there was little light inside the hallway. Dust and cobwebs snuffed out most of what was radiated by the solitary bulb still working in the chandelier hung from the ceiling. Bennett had more of an impression of what the place looked like than a clear, distinctive view. Shadows clung to its corners, filling them like piles of dust. The carpet was unidentifiable, probably more grime than fibres. He could feel his nostrils cloying with dust.

The old lady appeared from an open doorway. Music resonated from the room behind her. There was a smell of incense. Though normally Bennett despised such stuff he welcomed it now; it overpowered other odours, smells that were almost bad enough to make him nauseous. Perhaps that was why they burned joss sticks, dozens of which were scattered on shelves around the room. Books, mainly leather-bound editions, crinkly with age, shared space with them.

"You were at the park," the old lady said. Her voice had the same breathless whisper – which didn't surprise Bennett. What else could you expect in the kind of stale, dusty atmosphere of the house? It was a wonder they didn't asphyxiate. God alone knew what viruses were rampant here.

"He's come to apologise for what he said to us," the old man said. His hand, no more substantial than a bundle of dead leaves, pressed light against Bennett's shoulder, urging him into the room.

The old lady wore a floor length dress in a style Bennett recognised from the late sixties or early seventies. A hippy dress. Its colours had been dulled by time and dirt into monochrome. The old lady's arms were wrinkled sticks of bare flesh. Lead-coloured bangles hung from her wrists.

Both were barefooted, Bennett realised. Purple blotches, like diseased flesh, were the only colour. Their toenails were thick, like poorly preserved ivory, yellowed with age.

He swallowed back the bile that burned in his throat as he turned to face the old man, ready to tug the door open so his friends could enter.

Something, though, restrained him.

It wasn't compassion. Or fear of the consequences. By the time anyone found the old couple their bodies would have decomposed so much no trace of the men's presence would remain. Besides, they had no intention of leaving any evidence here.

"Would you care for a drink?" the old lady said.

Bennett stared at her. Now was the time to strike. He felt a burning outrage against them both, undiminished by meeting and talking to them. They epitomised everything that he hated.

Coming to a decision, Bennett turned to face the door when something heavy struck his head.

Hours later he awoke to the worst headache he had had in years. Worse than any hangover he had ever had too; he felt sick, uncomfortable, unable to move, and with a pulsing light inside his head that came with regular waves of pain.

Bennett's memories of what happened were vague. He could recall walking to the old couple's house. He could even remember stepping inside, and the smells and dust. The smells were still there, clogging his nostrils like rotting dough. Disgusted, Bennett opened his eyes; they were gritty with mucus and for a moment he could barely see anything other than the vague impression some distance away of a curtained window. Grunting, Bennett struggled to sit up, even though the pain inside his head worsened. He realised that his hands had been tied together. The coarse rope had already worn layers of skin from his wrists and hurt.

His ankles had been tied as well.

Sitting on a kind of low couch like a chaise longue, its upholstered seat was hard to his buttocks and uncomfortable. Finally, after a few minutes, Bennett managed to swivel round till his feet touched the carpet. By now he could make out more of his surroundings. The light came from a naked bulb hung from a plaster rose in the ceiling. Though large, the room was empty apart from the couch. A dim expanse of dull carpet lay between him and the window and he could hear an occasional scuffle inside the walls, either rats or mice. Other than this, the only sound was music, that infernal bloody sixties trash he had heard before, dimmed by distance.

As his mind grew clearer Bennett wondered if the couple had realised something was going on, though he could not imagine what could have warned them. What had happened to his friends? Even if he hadn't opened the door to them, they wouldn't have waited long before bursting in.

As if in answer he heard someone scream. It was a man, crying out in pain. The scream was stifled almost at once as if gagged.

Bennett raised his hands to his mouth and gnawed at the rope. He still had all his own teeth and they were strong and sharp; it did not take long before the rope's fibres parted beneath them, even though he hated the taste of oil and dust in which they had been smothered. It made him feel nauseous.

There was a series of loud bumps and someone laughed. It was neither Pinky nor Sam; perhaps the old man, he thought. Bennett tore away another mouthful of fibres from his bonds, spitting them out. He'd soon have the bastard laughing a different tune when he was free. His teeth dug into the rope once more, tearing at it in anger now.

Spurred on by more bumps, Bennett soon managed to weaken the rope till he could tear it apart. Throwing it onto the floor, he bent to unfasten the rope around his ankles. Seconds later he threw that away as well.

Taking a few deep breaths to calm his nerves, Bennett massaged his wrists to restore their circulation, then heaved himself off the couch, searching for anything he could use as a weapon. He pulled back the curtains from the window. Its old square panes were coated in layers of grime, though he could still see through them onto the back garden – an untidy jungle of overgrown evergreen bushes, most of them rhododendron black as grottoes. It stretched out for what had to be a hundred feet, possibly more.

Realising he was on the first floor, Bennett wondered how the old man and his wife had managed to haul him all the way upstairs; they had to be a lot stronger than either of them looked to move his weight. Frowning, Bennett returned to the couch. He tipped it over onto its side and started to work on one of its heavily carved wooden legs, forcing it back and forth to wrench it free. It was curved, narrowing to an ornate foot. The wood was heavy and hard. Finally he hefted the leg in one hand and took a couple of swings. It was no baseball bat but he knew it would be effective enough.

Breathing heavily, Bennett approached the door. It was

locked, as he'd expected. Belts and braces, Bennett thought. He tightened his grip on the couch leg. Much good their precautions would do once he was face to face with them and it would take more than a locked bedroom door to keep him here.

There were more bumps, louder this time. Putting his ear to the door Bennett could tell they came from further down the passage outside. With a grunt, he stepped back from the door, pounding into it as hard as he could with his shoulder. His breath exploded from his lungs and he winced in pain. The door was stronger than it looked. Like the old couple, he thought. Stepping back, he kicked as hard as he could with the sole of his shoe. The door shuddered and he heard something give. A splinter sprang from the doorframe next to its lock. He kicked it again, feeling the tendons inside his calf stretch painfully. He was getting too old for tricks like this, too old and too stiff. But this time, though, he could tell he had almost succeeded. He grabbed hold of the door handle and gave it a tug. There was a mournful creak and the door burst open. Bennett stepped outside in time to catch sight of the old man who had started down the passage from a door several yards away. Bennett ran towards him, brandishing the makeshift club. With a yelp, the old man ducked into the nearest room, but was too slow shutting the door against him. Bennett shouldered it open, gratified to hear the man fall across the floor behind it.

Sam lay inside the room on a bed, gagged and bound. The old lady was knelt over him. Something long and red, like an intravenous drip, hung from just below her mouth. It dangled on Sam's neck, and Bennett was disgusted to see what looked like a mouth at the very end of it open and shut as if it was trying to suck itself to his friend's skin.

Grunting with the exertion, Bennett swung the couch leg across the back of the old lady's head, felling her. He strode into the room, turned, saw the old man trying to scramble to his feet, nursing what looked like a broken arm; Bennett gave him no chance. Once, twice he swung the weapon, crushing his skull with resounding thuds. He felt something give at the second blow. A third followed, but by now the old man was on the floor, his legs twitching as if he was having a fit. Which, Bennett thought, debating whether to hit him again, he probably was. The bloody red vein beneath his mouth had been dislodged and lay on his collar. Something dark oozed from it.

Bennett turned to the man's wife. The single blow to her head seemed to have killed her. This didn't surprise him. It had been a hard one, delivered with all his weight behind it.

Throwing his weapon to one side, Bennett untied Sam's hands. Released, Sam tugged out the lump of cloth that had been bunged into his mouth.

"They've got Pinky in another room," he said, looking sick. "They started on him first. Did you hear the poor bastard?"

Bennett had had no idea which of them screamed. The sounds had been too wretched to tell.

Saying nothing, Bennett helped Sam up, then hurried into the room from which the old man had fled. Pinky was lying there, fastened like Sam on a bed. As soon as they saw their friend's face, though, they knew they were too late. Just as they could tell that Pinky had died in terror; it was transfixed on what was left of his features. Part of his face, though, had gone, as if a powerful acid had eaten it away to leave a gaping blood-soaked hole.

"The fucking bastards killed him," Sam muttered, though that was what they had come here to do to the couple.

Still struggling to understand how the couple had managed to overwhelm them, Bennett grunted. It just didn't seem possible. Just as it didn't seem possible that the old man had been responsible for the damage to Pinky's face.

"Did you see the thing hanging from the old woman when she was leaning over you? What the hell was it?"

Sam shuddered, gritting his teeth. "It was obscene." He looked as if he was going to be sick. "It couldn't have been real."

Bennett wasn't so sure. It had looked real to him, *too bloody real.*

They searched the room. There was little furniture inside it, a set of drawers and a cheap plywood wardrobe dating from sometime in the 1950s. They contained nothing more than a few sheets. No sign of any acid or anything else corrosive – or anything that might have been used to carve Pinky's face.

"What happened to the bits that are missing?" Bennett said.

Reluctantly, Sam looked again at their friend's body. Most of Pinky's nose and the whole of one side of his face had gone, as if scooped away.

"It must be somewhere," Bennett said.

But where? And why had the man done it?

"You don't think he ate it?"

"Ate it?" Bennett seriously wondered if his friend had been unhinged by what had happened.

Sam frowned. "Makes you wonder if they might have killed that lad the landlord told you about."

"If they did, why did they? And what did they do with the body?"

Sam shrugged. "Questions no one will answer now."

"I suppose not. We better get out of here."

"And Pinky?"

"Leave him here. It'll be ages before anyone investigates this place."

Already Bennett was working out what he and Sam would do once they left. They would return to his house, have a drink or two to relax their nerves, then make sure they had the same story. The less said the better.

Bennett grunted to himself. At least there'd be no more tramps sitting in the park. Having little empathy, even for his friends, he was not bothered by what had happened to Pinky. He was just one less person he could share his time with at the pub. Beyond that he knew he would barely miss him.

"What was that noise?"

There was a quaver in Sam's voice. Nerves, Bennett thought. He was always the weakest, always the one most ready to cut and run.

Annoyed, Bennett stopped and listened though.

Despite his scepticism, he could hear something too. Not loud, more a rustling, like stiff rushes.

They returned to the room in which Sam had been held. The old man's legs were still twitching. There were other movements too further up his body, beneath the cardigan on his chest. For the first time Bennett began to feel afraid. He could tell that these movements were wrong. There was no sense to them.

"What the hell is it?" Sam said, echoing his fears.

It was as if something – perhaps a lot of *somethings*, all small and spindly – were moving under the old man's clothes. Bennett snatched up the couch leg from where he had discarded it. He edged nearer the old man even though he wanted nothing more than to turn round and run.

"Don't." Sam whispered. "Leave it be."

But he couldn't. He couldn't just leave it. He had to see. With a certainty of movement that belied his fear, Bennett pressed the couch leg against the bottom of the old man's cardigan, using it to push the garment further up his chest. The wool caught on a splinter, making the task easier, till Bennett saw what he was exposing. Neither hard and straight like an insect's legs nor bonelessly muscular as in an octopus, the thick red tendrils writhed in the open air. They were long – longer than he had expected, with mouth-like suckers at their ends. One unexpectedly whipped out at him with uncanny accuracy and he flinched away from it, dropping the couch leg.

"Get out of here." Sam tugged his arm. As they turned, one of the tendrils sprang and coiled like a rusty bedspring around Sam's wrist, clenching tight. He cried out in pain and grabbed at it with his free hand, trying to take hold of it and tear it free, but his fingers could not get a grip on it.

"Help me," Sam cried. His face filled with terror. A second

tendril whipped out at him.

Bennett recoiled. Already he could see them climbing free of the old man's chest like a nest of spiders, all legs and no body. A deep cavity lay where they had been. He could see the old man's ribs inside it.

"Help me," Sam pleaded. He tugged at the tendrils, but more of them were fastening themselves to him all the time. They were ridiculously long, as thick as a man's middle fingers, and tough, covered in a kind of carapace. Bennett looked for something other than the couch leg with which to defend himself, but there was nothing.

"I'll get something downstairs," Bennett said, "a knife."

Ignoring Sam's pleas Bennett fled from the room; the air quivered behind him. Tendrils snatched only inches from the back of his neck, trying to grasp him. Sam shouted, begging for him to stop but Bennett slammed the door shut. He ran to the stairs, stumbling down umpteen steps at a time till he reached the hallway. He did not stop till he had left the house and run on, staggering, past the park. Almost blind to everything around him he continued to the town centre, bumping past what few pedestrians there were and almost getting himself run over as he recklessly crossed road after road till he reached his home. Slamming and locking the door behind him, he leaned against it, gasping for breath. His chest hurt and he knew he had pushed himself to the brink of a heart attack. All but falling into his living room he poured himself a large brandy and gulped it down. It burned his throat but helped. He drank a second, more slowly this time as he sank onto the sofa, his hands still shaking. He could not believe what had happened. It was like a nightmare. He shut his eyes, unable to remove the sight of those hideous tendrils. He could see them lashing themselves round Sam's arms.

It was nearly an hour later as Bennett poured himself a fifth brandy when someone knocked on the door.

Spilling most of the alcohol on his lap, Bennett leapt to his feet.

"Bennett, you bastard, open this fucking door!"

It was Sam, his voice furious.

"You double-crossing cowardly bastard. Open this door or I'll kick it in."

Bennett scowled. No one had spoken to him like this for years.

Slamming his glass on the table Bennett strode to the door. What relief he felt at his friend having escaped was tempered by the man's anger. What right had he to accuse Bennett of anything?

Bennett swung the door open. Sam stood, dishevelled, his coat stained with blood.

"God, man, you look like you murdered someone. Get off the street, for heaven's sake. You'll get us arrested."

"Good of you to think of that." Sam's voice was sour. He pushed his way in and glanced at Bennett's brandy by the sofa. "See you wasted no time."

"Have one yourself. You look like you need it." Feeling his anger fade, Bennett followed him in.

Slumping onto an armchair, Sam reached for the brandy and poured it into an empty glass. His hands shook so much most of it slopped onto the carpet. Sam looked down at it and smiled. "Sorry about that, old man. It's been a trying night."

Bennett sat on the sofa.

"How did you escape?"

"Escape?" Sam grimaced as if the brandy tasted bad and put it down.

Bennett tensed, feeling uneasy as he studied his friend. Sam's coat was still dripping. The front of it was soaked with blood.

Sam glanced across at him and reached for the buttons down his coat. His fingers were red.

"It won't make much difference," Sam said as if this explained everything. "We can still continue just like before, only better, stronger."

Bennett's face drained of colour. He darted a look at the

door into the kitchen. He had knives in there, carving knives. If he reached them he could kill Sam with ease.

His friend grinned at him.

He pulled his coat open, popping buttons. Coiled like a bundle of dark red brambles, nesting tight against his chest, the creature stirred.

"Those old hippies were hard for them to work with," Sam said. "They had to be pushed and threatened, forced to kill. It went against their principles, you see, the soft old bastards. Damn near starved these creatures to death."

Bennett rose to his feet.

"It'll be easier with us. We don't mind killing, do we? We love it, in fact." Sam grinned. "There are benefits," he added. "Those hippy bastards were over a hundred years old, you know. You wouldn't have guessed it, would you? They were, though. It's quid pro quo, don't you see? There's a payoff. Benefits. Benefits in kind, I suppose. Things work both ways. No more aches and pains. No more muscles creaking with old age. No more bones turning fragile as the years pass by. We'd feel young again, Bennett. *Young and strong.*"

Bennett looked at his friend's chest. The blood was already beginning to clot. There was barely any sign of what hid inside other than a vein pulsing across his chin.

Bennett stared at the creature on Sam's blood-soaked lap. It was already starting to straighten its legs.

Sam's grin broadened.

Lightning Source UK Ltd.
Milton Keynes UK
UKOW040712200912

199330UK00001B/4/P